OFF THE BEATEN PATH

SIENNA EGGLER

BENEKEID INK, LLC

ALSO BY EGGLER

Fluid Bonding

In the Company of Wolves

The Threads That Weave

Voracity

Early Adopter

Early Adopter

The Celeste Files

Last Train Home

Off the Beaten Path

This Hole Was Made For (You And) Me

Speaking Out In Silence

Learn more at www.siennaeggler.com/books/

BAYETTEK
DOYEMERE
LEXANARD
Ashfort
SILVERSTONE MINE
REDADORE
Saincaster
FLOWER FIELDS
Zachick
LAEFORD
Candle Cove
CLARK MEADOWS.
RAGING RIVER
CALDERA SEA
N
E
S
W

Contents

1

ANYWHERE BUT HERE

Meike had been out of college for all of two months, and already their parents were making plans to renovate. Not that they blamed them; the room was going to be vacant until at least the end of the year, possibly more. It all depended on whether Meike could tolerate working on a farm. If not, there was always horticulture.

They knelt before their bookcase, an old hand-me-down that once belonged to their mother. Solid wood and towered a good six feet above them. Heavy, and heavier still, with a collection of fiction books and a smattering of encyclopedias and dictionaries.

They'd collected a ton of knickknacks and toys over the years, the bulk of which they discarded without a second thought. But even with their e-reader, it was hard to just toss books. There was something special about the weight and feel of a book, and the satisfying sound of pages turning.

"Meike. *Meike.*"

They turned from the looming shelf to meet their mother's stern gaze. "Always got your heads in the clouds," she said, exasperated. "I asked you to sort this out a month ago." She didn't so much as ask than demanded, as they recalled. But they knew better than to talk back.

"I had a good idea of what I want to keep and donate. It'll only take thirty minutes."

Thirty minutes to box up their whole life and move across the country. The host family supposedly had a small shelf set up for them, but Meike intended to pack light. Two suitcases and a backpack for their electronics would suffice.

Meanwhile, their bedroom for the past ten years was almost entirely stripped of character. Their desk was the first to go, dresser second, and old band and movie posters tossed, leaving faint imprints of what once was. All that remained was the bed and tv.

"You know you don't have to do this," she said. "You can stay here. I'm sure they'll give you your job back if you explain the situation."

"Can, don't want to." They'd given up on selling botany as a science to family; it always came back to retail gardens and floral shops. And they didn't want to be stuck in the same job they started in high school forty years later.

"Gabby, are you out your mind? We just got rid of the boys."

Meike was glad to have the heat taken off of them, but dad was...overly enthusiastic about them leaving, to put it lightly.

"I wasn't happy about that either."

He shooed her off to the side, a tape measure in hand. "We got you a sewing room, and I'm getting my man cave."

"Thanks, dad," they said flatly. He could at least pretend to care, but dad was never one to pull his punches, even with his kids.

"When are you leaving again? Two days?"

"Two weeks."

Dad raised an eyebrow. "... How much is it gonna take to get you out of here in a week?"

"Darius!" Mom rounded on him, a deep scowl on her face.

"I've never gotten to ride on an actual train before," they said before mom could squash the offer. Or any train, really.

Their hometown didn't have a subway system or any form of public transit. Cars were king here, though there was a tiny airport that could fly you to a real one in the neighboring city.

"What, Amtrak?" Dad pretended to think it over. "It's a slow ride, and you may be stuck there for two or three days, but..." He rubbed his chin, making Meike sweat for it. "I can work with that."

"Thanks, dad!"

"No problem, pumpkin."

"Darius! Stop running our children off," mom snapped.

Ignoring her, he turned to face the room. "I'm gonna put the 50 inch right here," he gestured to the spot currently occupied by the bed. "And my recliner right over here."

Meike pulled an encyclopedia from the shelf. "What even is a man cave?"

"A place where a man is free to be himself," he said. "Could be a game room, private theater, or a place to store his impressive comic book and gun collection."

"This fool just wants to play video games," mom huffed. "Which is fine by me. I need to be able to watch my programs."

They picked up a game guide to a jrpg they hadn't played in years. Most of the game took place in dungeons, the only reprieve being excursions into settlements to stock up on supplies and recruit new characters when the others eventually died.

The whole point of the game was to map out new areas and explore the range of classes while doing so. Could prove for an excellent time sink, though they were hoping to sneak in time to play their favorite MMO.

The latest expansion was announced a few months ago, one boasting an array of new classes and unexplored terrain. And, naturally, the release date was when Meike started work—on an organic farm with an "emergency" internet connection. Their host, Hakeem, essentially bragged about his kids being free from the influence of social media and television.

Meike sighed and placed the guide in the keep pile. They were going to be horribly under-leveled by the time they had a steady internet connection, but volunteering would look good on their resume.

They moved past the haphazardly stacked game guides to their reference books—plants to avoid, herbal remedies, and a comprehensive book on mushroom hunting. This latter book was dog-eared and falling apart, but Meike sorted it into the keep pile. Were there better and newer editions? Yes. But it was theirs, a gift and part of their initiation to the local mushroom society.

'A month isn't nearly enough,' they thought, glancing once more at the shelf, the sound of bickering in their ears.

"We're going to miss you, Capsule!"

"Have fun, Capsule!"

All early cries of farewell, all addressed to the avatar they piloted in the game; a spellcaster named Capsule, who provided heals, supportive skills, and offense in the form of familiars.

'They don't even know your name,' Meike thought, with a touch of bitterness. And not for a lack of interest; it just never came up. They considered the people in the group chat to be allies and acquaintances, but the word "friend" never came into consideration.

So to "EagerReaver" and "prostate_milk" they were simply "Capsule".

They sent a half-hearted assurance that they wouldn't be entirely off the grid. In a pinch, they could connect via hotspot, though it wasn't optimal for anything other than crafting and gathering. And all their social interaction came from raids...

Meike sighed and closed out of the app, their appetite for idle conversation lost. Just them, the train, and the other passengers, deeply engrossed in their smartphones and laptops. An odd person or two held a tablet or e-reader in their hands.

It was comforting, in a way, to be surrounded by people who didn't know their name or recent diagnosis. People who would assume they were merely shy or introverted. Meike tried telling someone they once saw as the closest thing to a friend, and her response was lukewarm at best.

The conversation quickly changed to the best place to farm mugwort, or some other middling herb. It was a better response than the one they feared, but left them feeling just as hollow.

'You're overthinking it, is all,' they tried to tell themself. That was the default stance for when things got to be too much, a brief stop on the road to a full shut down.

It was a bit late for regrets, but sometimes they wondered if this gig was even a good idea. Staying with a family they didn't know, for essentially free labor—"We'll pay you in experience!"—World Wide Opportunities on Organic Farms or "WWOOF" would look good on their resume.

Meike curled up on their window seat to admire the passing scenery. They loved road trips as a kid; seeing rows of green, horses, livestock, and the occasional body of water made the pain of confinement bearable. More so when they had a good book or music to occupy themself. And they wanted to enjoy every second, before retiring to their private room (dad was generous).

If they closed their eyes and tried to focus on the soft thunks of the train on track, they could almost feel themself slipping away into a light sleep.

The inevitable jolt came from the person a few seats away, a woman with long, white blonde hair. She'd let out an ear piercing laugh and drawn the ire from other passengers. Meike was mildly curious, but happy to stay in their own lane. Aside from staff, they were the only black person on board and didn't want to risk drawing attention to themself.

Things quieted down shortly after, and they diverted their attention back to the view outside. An endless stream of trees passed them by, but they spied hints they were in the Carolinas: Magnolia trees, Palmettos, the invasive kudzu species...But also home to Dionaea muscipula, or Venus flytraps. Difficult to care for, but a delight to observe.

Meike snapped a few pictures, wincing at the soft clicks of confirmation. They silenced their phone and resumed taking pictures, both of the plants and local wildlife. Folks in the group chat might enjoy it, or at least pretend to.

They were angling for a quick shot of a peculiar formation when the train hit a rough patch. In the midst of a cacophony of screams, Meike felt themself knocked off their chair and plunged into a world of blackness. The last photo they took was a circle of yellow mushrooms.

2

REALITY BITES

When they came to, it was not in the comfortable window seat, or even on the floor, in a spill of limbs and mass confusion. But a scene that felt right at home in a dream: a field of flowers and a setting sun.

Meike sat up with a yawn, more curious than anything. Nothing felt out of the ordinary with their body, but assuming the train crashed, there was no sign on it. No broken machinery, scorched tracks, or even the bodies of their fellow passengers. *'So it has to be a dream,'* they thought, and stood to take stock of their surroundings.

The field they'd found themself in consisted almost entirely of ranunculus flowers of all shades, but arranged in such a pleasing matter that it had to be deliberate. Someone's private garden, if they had to guess. And yet there was no sign of civilization anywhere, no houses, roads, or other structures. *'It's a dream.'*

But Meike had no love for buttercups, or the yellows and oranges that dotted the reds and blues. They cared little for flowers at all, outside of studying their properties and breeding potentials. Any garden of theirs, fictional or otherwise, would be strictly carnivorous: sundews, flytraps, pitcher plants, rafflesia, and waterwheels.

They waded through the flowers, their target the lone tree in the area. If they could climb it and get a good view, it might shed some light on this mystery. *'Or you'll fall down, hit your head, and wake up.'*

But Meike never got that far; they were in the middle of swinging themself up onto one of the sturdier branches, when their foot caught on something solid. Not solid the way the tree trunk was, but more of the flesh and bone variety. They tentatively nudged the object beneath the leaves, and something white and slender rolled out—a human arm.

They glanced around, half-expecting someone to rise above the flowers and aim an accusatory finger at them, before emitting a dull scream like a pod person. But no such scene followed. The only sound was the wind, birdsong, and the soft groans beneath their foot.

Meike crouched down and brushed the mass of dead leaves and flowers away from the arm, and froze when it grabbed for them. At least now they knew it was attached to someone, and not simply tossed out like day old bread. They frantically shook the hand off and resumed digging.

A jacket and another arm came into view, and with nails black with soil, Meike grasped the flailing hands and dug their heels into the ground. They weren't particularly strong; years of gaming, reading, and gardening only amounted to muscle memory and toned fingers, but determination guided them through.

Out popped a gasping figure, blonde hair almost indistinguishable from the dirt she was born from. The woman came kicking and sobbing, and dropped to her hands and knees in a patch of purple buttercups.

Meike stood back and watched as she hacked up soil, so thick and generous they almost mistook it for vomit. Next came chunks of leaves, and tiny, pink chunks they recognized as earthworms. She lowered her head into a clean section of the flowers once her gut was empty, and divulged into tears, great wracking sobs and disjointed concerns about her location and what became of the train and everyone else.

"I don't know," was all they could offer. They were just as lost, and horrified that this was, in fact, reality, and not a cozy dream.

"I know you. You were on the train…"

"Really, now? Cause I don't remember you."

Meike eyed her dirty blonde hair. "I keep to myself. But you were—" Loud. "Laughing," they said, with better tact than their mind.

"Anyway, my name is Anniken." She rolled her eyes. "But not like the child murderer." Too many overzealous space opera fans, it seemed.

"I've never seen it," Meike said, but never would dare to mock someone over their given name. Or care, really. They got enough flack for their own.

Everyone always assumed it was "Micah" or "Myka" until they learned the correct spelling. Same pronunciation, but mom wanted something "different," something to contemplate dad's very German surname.

Anniken spat a mouthful of black viscous fluid, a remainder of her earlier ordeal. "How is that even possible? Everyone has seen it."

"There are people without access to running water or even electricity," they said, and she went silent.

There was a good five minutes of blissful silence, during which Meike bemoaned the loss of their electronics and bags. The novelty of this bizarre detour was starting to wear off.

"So, like, you think this is purgatory?"

"Whatever it is, it's peaceful." What if they never got to play video games again? "But I could see how it could get boring."

"Have you seen anyone else?"

There seemed to be no end to the flower fields, and Meike was getting hungry. Their last "meal" was a Snickers bar. "Maybe they're all buried, like you." Or they turned up somewhere better, somewhere with food and running water.

"I almost died, you know." She stopped to hack up something awful. Anniken scrubbed most of the grime and dirt off with the flowers and a little spit shine, but was very much rough around the edges. But pretty despite it.

"Yeah, I was there."

"You're very nonchalant, aren't you?"

Meike shrugged. Their mom constantly reminded them of that throughout their childhood, and it came up during the screening process. "I think I see the way out," they said, pointing past a sloping hill. The flowers gave way to lush grass, and if they stared hard enough, a winding road. Question was, which way should they go?

They looked to Anniken for advice, but she looked just as confused. "We should go north. Always go north when you're lost."

"Do you get lost a lot?"

She gave an exasperated sigh. "Only twice. Once while hiking, the other backpacking—in Europe," she added. "I always keep a compass on me." She produced it now, and Meike felt a pang of jealousy.

It was a long road, and much like the flower fields, there seemed to be no end in no sight. The low grass on either side gradually became wilder until thick branches crisscrossed above, blocking out most of the sun.

Meike swatted a clump of leaves out of their face. "Are you sure we're going the right way?"

"You're free to turn back," she snapped. "The only way for me is forward."

They scuffed the ground with their sneakers. They'd been walking for what felt like hours, and had yet to see a river or a good stopping point. 'Maybe it really is purgatory...'

And suddenly Anniken was sprinting off without them. Meike struggled to keep up; exhaustion and hunger held them back as much as their low stamina. They had to double up to catch their breath and saw nothing but spots as she cooed and fawned over...

"—a dog!"

"Wait."

Meike sighed and flopped on the side of the road. The trees weren't as thick in this area, providing patches of bare sky—no longer a pale blue but a deepening purple. Darkness was quick on their heels and the odds of finding a place for the night were against them.

But Anniken was too busy fussing over...a corgi? Meike rubbed their eyes to make sure they weren't seeing things.

It was larger than average, with orange fur, and carried an adorable axe on its back. It bared its fangs at Anniken, who was ignoring the fundamental rule of strange dogs.

"What are you doing out here all alone, little guy," she said, in a sickeningly sweet baby voice. The dog growled and stepped back. "Is your owner nearby?" She glanced back at Meike. "See, I knew we were in the right direction! He'll take us to his owner and we'll go somewhere with a warm bed and food..."

"You shouldn't," they said, between gasps for air.

"It's okay. We aren't going to hurt you, little fella." She reached for the dog again, but this time it didn't move, only stood its ground and watched her with wary eyes. "Easy…" Her hand lowered to a spot behind the dog's ear, and it snapped back.

It moved so fast Meike only saw the results—the snarling dog, and Anniken's wide-eyed stare. And the blood running down her arm and pooling in her sleeve.

"Don't fucking patronize me," a gruff voice said.

By process of elimination, it could only be the dog. And while Meike was still processing this and the extent of Anniken's injuries, her shrill screams pierced the air.

3

ATOMIC DOG

The latest addition to the party left Meike deeply conflict-ed. They wanted to hug him and give him all the pets, but they didn't want to end up like Anniken, either. Her hand was half-wrapped in her jacket, concealing the open wound. And quietly sobbing, not from the pain, but her missing finger tip, which Meike suspected was somewhere in the dog's lower intestine by this point. They'd searched for a good ten minutes before he urged them on.

He glanced back at them, and Meike fought back the impulse to "d'aww".

"You kittens got a name?"

"I'm Meike," they said, when the dog pulled his lips from his teeth. How could something so cute be so mean?

"What about you, whitey?"

"Go fuck yourself," she spat.

He turned back to the road and took off on a light trot, claws clicking against the brick road. "Whitey it is, then!"

Meike jogged after him. "I thought dogs couldn't see certain col-ors." They knew enough to know dogs weren't color blind, just lim-ited.

"And until today, you didn't know we could talk, either! Some of us, anyway."

So there was hope of meeting a genuine good boy, after all. "Is that axe real, or just for show?"

"It's not for chopping firewood, I'll tell you that."

Anniken tugged on Meike's hoodie. "Why are you chatting that damn thing up? Did you see what he did to my hand?"

"It'll be fine," they said. "We'll patch it up at the village." Meike had no way of knowing that for sure, but knew they didn't want to be alone in the dark, either.

"And you trust it?" She pointed at the dog with her good hand.

"I have a name," he said. "It's Pickles. Pickles Barkenshire Jr. Don't call me a 'thing' or an 'it,' and I won't call you a *bitch*."

"Fuck you."

Meike stepped between her and the dog. "This wouldn't have happened if you asked before petting him."

She grumbled an apology, and the group continued on. Pickles insisted they hurry before it got too dark out, and they had no doubt he would ditch them at the first sign of trouble.

"Also, how do you know English?"

"English? Is that what you call your dialect?"

"No, it's a language. One of the biggest in the world," Anniken said, rolling her eyes.

"Never heard of it," he huffed. "Maybe you come from some secluded part of Glasend, kitten. But here, we speak *Glaes*, the bastardized tongue of the common folk."

"Look, dog—"

"Pickles."

"Pickles, will you be a good boy and help us out?"

He stopped and pawed at his muzzle. "You got money?"

"What do you need with money? You don't even have thumbs."

Meike nudged her in the side. "I have $80 in cash on me, but I don't think my card is useful here."

"You're gonna want coin. Gold, silver, copper...not for me, but yourselves." He waved a paw in the air. "I can show you to an inn, but you're on your own after that."

"What about you," Meike said. "Where are you going?"

"Worry about yourself, kid."

He led them to a large stone building with a thatched roof; a structure right out of a medieval movie set. Bundles of straw littered the area in front of a small barn, and odd "street lamps" flanked the entrance to the inn. They tapped one of them while waiting for Pickles to summon the innkeeper.

"Kerosene lanterns..." Dismay was quietly building within them. And the windows, as far as they could see, were similarly lit. No electricity, phones, or wifi.

"Watch yourself," an old lady said, squinting at them from the dimly lit doorway.

Meike wanted to slink off and make themself scarce, but Anniken kept a firm hand on their hoodie, ready to gag them if necessary.

"We need a room for the night," Anniken said. "Two, if you can spare them."

The innkeeper eyed them up and down, no doubt curious about the strange attire of the two guests. Or just questioning what they'd gotten themself into. She herself wore a faded brown dress and dirty apron, her hair pulled back into a tight bun and covered by a white cap.

Contrast that with Anniken and Meike's colorful jackets, jeans, and sneakers, and they looked like a pair of clueless tourists.

"And do you have a shower or something?" Anniken combed a leaf and clump of soil from her hair. "I had a...very unfortunate accident."

"I don't think they have that here," Meike hissed. Unless the oil lamps were just an aesthetic choice, Anniken was out of luck.

"I don't know what this 'shower' is, but we could boil some water for you. It'll be extra, I'm afraid."

"I'm sorry, what?" She looked at Pickles. "She's joking, right?"

"They don't have running water," they whispered, right as the innkeeper was responding.

"Take it or leave it. This isn't the royal palace, princess."

They tugged on her arm. "What are you gonna do?" Never mind the bath; they didn't have proper money.

"Fine. But I also hope you can understand that we are three travelers down on our luck, and won't be able to pay for the night—"

The innkeeper was fast, and would've shut the door on them had Pickles not stopped it with a paw.

Anniken mouthed a "thank you" to the dog and braced her foot against the door. "You aren't seriously going to us out in the dark, are you? What if we're attacked by bandits?"

"No money, no service," she said, and struggled to push against their combined forces.

"What if we promised to do some work for you," Meike offered.

"No deal!"

"What's your damage, lady," Anniken said, and pressed her weight into the door. One good kick and the old woman would go flying.

"I'll cry for help if you don't back off," she snarled. "I've got a sleeping knight upstairs. Don't think he's not afraid to set you upstarts straight."

Pickles whined and flattened his belly against the ground, staring at her with imploring eyes.

"...Oh, you poor dear. I do hate to see small dogs sleeping like hogs." She bared her teeth at Anniken. "You and your friend can stay in the barn if you're so insistent. But I'll make sure your little doggie is taken care of." That last sentence came out sickeningly sweet.

"No deal," Anniken said, but stumbled back as Pickles withdrew his paw and darted inside with a series of excited yips. "Wait!" The door slammed shut, and she fell upon it, banging her fists and cursing the innkeeper in what Meike understood to be German. Meike had to drag her off.

"That flea-bitten mutt just threw us under the bus! Bastard!"

"Forget him," they said. "What about us?" They were tired, hungry, and already missing the mundane comfort of toilet paper.

The barn wasn't Meike's ideal resting place. There were three horses, a cow, and two pigs on the bottom floor. The only viable sleeping spot was the hayloft, a pile of moldy hay pushed back into a corner.

Not even Anniken had the energy to march outside and pick a fight with the manager. After allowing herself a few whispered obscenities, she curled up on a dry pile of hay. Meike followed shortly, having swept the barn for any other signs of life.

4

THE DAILY GRIND

"Oh, dear…how did this happen?"

Anniken winced as the makeshift bandage, something Meike made on a whim, was peeled off. The skin beneath was pale and scarred, but the most notable feature was her shortened middle finger.

"Dog bite," she said, and glared at the space at Meike's feet. The culprit in question had slunk off after leading them to the herbalist, known simply as Griselda.

She had a small pop up shop in a quiet corner of the market square. Odd bottles and herbs lined the shelf behind her, and there was a mortar and pestle resting on the counter. She'd been working at it when they approached her, and Meike was curious to know more. But Anniken came first.

"Do you think it was rabid?"

"No, just an asshole."

Griselda uncapped a tiny bottle and sprinkled clear liquid onto Anniken's finger. "No sign of infection either, I'm happy to say. But in the future, I would recommend seeking help within a few hours. Sooner, if possible. Otherwise reattachment is nigh impossible."

"We lost her finger," Meike said.

"Pity, that. I'm afraid I can't do anything more than speed up the healing process."

"It's no problem," Anniken said, turning away. "I'm left handed."

Meike stood on their tiptoes to get a better look at a round bottle at the very top of the shelf, filled with a teal liquid. "Do you have potions? And what kind?"

She clucked her tongue. "One question at a time, child." Funny, coming from her; Meike guessed her to be in her thirties. Her skin was wrinkle free and black hair was free of gray. But the way she carried herself gave her the air of someone beyond their years.

Or it was just a facade to help boost sales.

"There are ways of restoring your finger, but I don't offer that service. You'd need a mage, but because it's such a small thing, the fee would be less."

"How much? I can barely afford to pay you."

"Oh, I wasn't going to charge you." Griselda honed her gaze on Meike and they shifted in place. "You two aren't from here, are you?"

"We're from far away," Anniken said. "We were stranded after our ship washed up on shore, so we're looking for work until we can find a way back." She was quick on her feet, something Meike admired about her.

"If you're looking for work, there are always requests on the market board. Laborers, housekeepers, cooks…there's something for everyone."

Meike's hand shot into the air. "What about apprentices?"

Griselda cocked her head to the side. "Ambitious one, aren't we? You'll have a harder time with that one, unless some kind soul takes pity on you."

"I was actually thinking I could work for you? I majored in…I studied…" Their hands waved wordlessly in the air.

"They studied at an elite college for botanists, a class of people who research flora and fauna. It's a very practical field, so while Meike is familiar with the relevant plants, they're completely lacking in magical ability." Anniken gave them a thumbs up.

"Nice sales pitch," they said, and they meant that sarcastically, but to their ears sounded like the sad mewling of a starving cat.

"So you know the ins and out, then?"

"I know the fundamentals," they said. "And I'm a fast learner." They could identify healing herbs and had a good idea of how to use a mortar and pestle. It was all grinding and tossing everything into boiling water, or adding a small amount to make a cream.

"While I personally don't take on apprentices, I could use some help around my shop." She nodded behind them. "My main shop. I usually hire out help to deliver larger orders in and out of the city. Do you know your way around Laeford?"

The city of Laeford was large, unpredictable, and its inhabitants weren't always human. Pickles gave Meike and Anniken a quick tour on the way to the market, but they could barely remember their way back, let alone the architecture or shop fronts.

"I'm good with directions and I know the major highlights, yes."

"We'll give you a trial run. How does that sound?"

Anniken flexed her hand and inspected the freshly healed wound. She clapped that same hand on Meike's shoulder and pulled them into an awkward side hug. "They'll do it! Won't you, Meike?"

They couldn't tell if she was being menacing or friendly, but nodded in agreement. "I won't let you down, Griselda!"

"Hm, yes. You're going to want to do something about your clothes first. Both of you—you look like marks."

"It's on the to-do list," Anniken said. "Like I said, we're in a hard spot."

"Oh, I can spare something for this one. But you, you're on your own."

"Oh nein…"

The request board was a mess of recent requests plastered over and among faded and peeling parchment. They ranged from simple: *Missing dog found,* to complex, *Adventurers needed for an expedition into the Silverstone Mines! We're taking it BACK from the kobolds! Serious inquiries only! This is NOT a training exercise!*

"It's like a video game," Meike said, admiring the rough sketch of a dragon.

"A video game without respawns, maybe." Anniken sighed and tugged on one flyer. "I'm not cut out for any of this. I'm a software developer."

"I'm sure you can do something related to…" Their eyes fell on the drawing of a funky looking mushroom and beneath it, a timid call for foragers. "Annie, you do a lot of hiking."

"For fun, not as a living."

They showed her the flyer, but she barely glanced at it. "Look, mushroom hunting is fun. I don't know how much it pays, but it must be decent if they can't do it for themself." It almost made them want to ditch the job for Griselda and go frolic in the forest. At least then they'd have something concrete, but they had to stay focused on the bigger picture.

"Foraging isn't the same as hiking. And I try not to deviate off the established paths. Unlike my brothers…" Meike perked up; she barely talked about herself, and she never explained why she was even in the US. Sightseeing seemed most likely. "And I know nothing about mushrooms aside from portobellos and shiitake."

"I could teach you! I've gone hunting a few times, and so far this world mirrors our own, in terms of flora and fauna. It's the people that are…" They turned to Pickles, for example.

Now that they were in the city proper, the dog stood upright, a small humanoid. But there were others like him, tall dog-like men that would be right at home in a furry convention. And then there were the lizard people, and people with the claws and discreetly folded wings of birds.

"Weirdos, I know." She pinched the bridge of her nose. "And you expect me to run errands for them?"

"It's not easy on me either, you know." Meike had no home to go back to, and what quiet corners they could find were spent in silent rumination. "We'll just have to make the best of it until we sort things out."

"And what if we never do? What then?"

Meike shrugged and quickly stepped back as a bulky, reptilian creature strode up to the board and plucked a flyer with his tongue, like a frog snatching a fly out of the air. It left just as quickly as it came, dragging a long tail behind. It vaguely reminded them of a leopard gecko, though it was hard to say for sure since it wore a long green cloak.

They turned back to Anniken, who'd buried her face in her hands. "I guess we adapt? The other option isn't so nice."

"I hate it here," she said, peeking at them between her fingers. "I'm this close to losing my shit, Meike."

"So we'll find you a job with humans." They checked the board again and grimaced. On the plus side, she was more less likely to have a non-human employer. "Look, this is a *Laetiporus*, one of many shelf fungi commonly found on trees. Most people refer to it as 'chicken of the woods' because, well, it tastes like chicken!" They waved the flyer under her nose until she took it.

"Why do know so much about mushrooms?" She wrinkled her nose at them, which was a step up from despair. "I thought you were a plant nerd."

"Botany isn't just about plants! We even study algae."

"Give it to me," Pickles said, standing on the tips of his toes and waving a paw at Anniken. "Don't know much 'bout shrooming, but you notice a lot from this height."

"Fine, you take it. I need something more…respectable."

Pickles snatched the paper out of the air and sat back on his haunches to look it over. Not being able to pet him was pure agony, but Meike managed somehow. "When does your new job start?"

"…We haven't worked that out yet." They moved away from the board to cast their shadow over the dog, leaving Anniken to squint and sigh. "She just said she'd call me when she was ready, but I'm hoping sometime this week." How she would pull that off, they had no idea.

"It's best to keep your options open," he said, handing the flyer back. "I always have at least three jobs going."

"Doing what?" Emotional support murder hobo?

"Herding, fightin', killing rats." He wiggled his paws and Meike saw the small toes were slender digits, toe beans and all. "Adventuring is where the real money is, but you know how it is."

"I actually don't."

"I'm small," he said.

"Oh, right…"

"People don't take you seriously unless you're big and mean. Small and cute? Come on!"

"I can relate," they said, crouching down to his level. "But I'm hoping to start over here."

He patted them on the head. "You remind me of myself when I was a pup." He tugged on invisible suspenders. "I was a sailor. Well, a pirate, but still."

"I was a loner, I guess." By habit, not design. "Uni was…awkward, but it can't be any worse than this." It was a step up, really. Meike didn't go to any wild parties and barely hung around the fringes of a group or two.

He slapped them on the shoulder. "That's the spirit!"

Anniken rejoined them shortly after, grim faced and sober. "I found something I can tolerate."

"What is it?" They tried to get a good look at the listing, but she folded it in half.

She sighed. "One of the most under-appreciated jobs in the world."

"Housekeeping?"

"Close," she said. "Cashiering."

5

A KINDRED SPIRIT ON SINNET STREET

Meike didn't start work until several days later, and only after Pickles pestered them into confronting Griselda.

"Oh right," she'd said, a dreamy look in her eyes. "I did promise to give you a try, did I not?"

They'd almost burst into tears at the frustration of it all; it would've been a safer bet to take up the shrooming job. But Griselda gave them a tattered old cloak to cover their otherworldly garments, and a leather satchel of goods. Nothing fragile, thankfully, but a series of creams, powdered mixes, and herbs.

These they could readily identify, but not the strange markings scratched into the strips of leather clinging to individual orders. Griselda's personal system, they wagered, and only she had the key.

Every minute they spent being brought up to speed drove a pin of regret in their heart, but it all seemed less scary after, and now that they had Pickle's help with the lay of the land.

"I'll only help you this once," he said. Pickles squinted at the key sheet, written in Griselda's scrawling handwriting. "You're looking for Hollow's End, which is near the shady side of the city."

"Shady as in trees, right?"

Pickles wrinkled his upper lip in response.

"...Shady as in trees, right?"

Small as he was, they were glad to have him by their side. Hollow's End was crawling with people Meike could only describe as "suspect," the sort who shrouded themself in dark cloaks and hoods and carried concealed weapons. It was dark, yes, but the street didn't look any different from the ones they'd seen so far. The main difference was the lack of people, or small groups that idled together on doorstops.

"Don't look like a mark," Pickles said, swatting them on the hip when they paused to stare at a tavern named Hog's End. The petrified head of a pig hung from the heavy wooden door.

They fought the urge to check the satchel. Losing their shipment was a good way to get fired, maybe even lose their life, if Griselda was the sort to take it that far. But she surely wouldn't trust a novice with anything worth losing, right?

"What's the name?"

"Um..." Meike nervously glanced from side to side as they fished out the paper. "It just says Remy, but I don't know who or what to look for."

"You're lucky you have me," he grumbled. "I know of Remy, but he's not the sort of guy you wanna get mixed up with."

"Is he an assassin," they whispered. And here they were, transporting poisons for his latest victim.

"Worse. He's a skirt chaser."

They glanced down at their jeans, obscured by the cloak. "I don't wear skirts."

"...Just let me do the talkin', will ya?" He adapted a little swagger, which Meike supposed he thought of as his "tough guy" walk. They tried not to giggle. And if it didn't fool them, it wouldn't fool Remy, either. But they let him take the lead to a small shop on the corner.

A topless lizard woman leaned against the wall, and Meike avoided looking at her while Pickles scratched at the door. Anywhere but here was their mood at the moment, but they had a job to do.

Thankfully, the man who answered the door looked very human and lacked fangs. He yawned and brushed his bangs from his red-rimmed eyes. "Cripes, it's not even noon yet! Whaddya want?"

"We're here on behalf of Lady Griselda," Pickles said, and the man paled. "An anti-itch salve, I imagine?"

"You shut your mouth," he hissed, and slammed the door.

"*Pickles!*"

"He'll be back," he said, grinning wildly.

The man reappeared a few moments later for the exchange. "I pay a high price for discretion, but maybe I should take my patronage elsewhere." He snatched the pouch of powder and flung a handful of silver coins at Meike.

"Please don't," they said. "Pickles is just helping me get familiar with the area."

Remy raised his eyebrows and looked Meike up and down. They shifted beneath their cloak and willed the ground to open up beneath them. "Eh, as long as you don't announce my business to the world, I don't care who you are. But you." He pointed at Pickles. "Can make tracks."

Pickles dropped on all fours and shook his bottom at the man, tail aggressively wagging in the air.

"Ugh," Remy cried, and placed a hand against his forehead. "No class! No class at all," he said, and closed the door.

"That wasn't *too* bad," Meike said, once Remy's and Hollow's End was far behind them.

"Look, kid, you might be better off picking flowers." He was going through the rest of the orders. "Hollow's End is probably as bad as it gets, but what if she wants you to branch out?"

"I handled it just fine." Finding people and locations was their biggest obstacle, but those things worked out with practice. "And this will help with my apprenticeship."

"Somehow I doubt that." He tapped a claw against his teeth. "You should've tried setting up with the white one."

"Her name's Anniken."

"Yeah, the white one." He handed back their precious code sheet. "The others are pretty straightforward and in safer areas, but I can't guarantee the people are any better."

"...You aren't leaving me, are you?"

Pickles sat on his haunches and stared back at them, his expression indiscernible. "I can point you in the right direction for one more, but then I want to be on my own."

"Alright..."

"Meike, I'm doing this out of the kindness of my heart. If you want this job, you gotta put yourself out there."

"And I have a map." Which they could barely read, but he didn't need to know that.

His expression went blank again. "What street intersects with Sinnet, then?"

"Um...I can't tell you without looking at it, but I know where it is."

"Sure you do." He sighed. "It's near the statue of a mermaid, down by the docks. If you ever get confused, forget the street names and look for landmarks."

"I can do that," they said, bouncing on their feet and eager to start.

"Great! You do that and I'll treat you to a steak dinner as a reward. How does that sound?"

They stopped bouncing. "I'm a vegetarian."

"Two steaks for me and a veggie strudel for you!"

It took some time, but Meike found two of their clients. Cream and a pouch of herbs for a man with a heavily scarred face, and powder for a self-entitled "crone in training." That left a small pouch of herbs for the resident on Sinnet Street.

This one gave them the least amount of trouble. Meike wasn't the best at finding their way through unfamiliar territory, but with Pickles' tips and the knowledge of the docks, they followed the signs—the gradually sloping street, the loitering sailors, and the unmistakable stench of fish and cries of gulls.

The mermaid statue stood out like a sore thumb, a lovingly crafted and erotic figure. But the body wasn't quite right; unlike the classical mermaids they were used to, this one would belong in a low budget horror movie. It was mostly humanoid in nature, with gills, webbed fingers and ears, a row of shark-life teeth, and what appeared to be seaweed dangling from its head. A long tail extended beyond its thighs, ending in a fin riddled with barnacles. Meike glanced away from the statue's heavy bosom, to the group of small children splashing in the fountain below.

Very human children, given their clear lack of fur, tails, or claws, a fact cemented by them turning their play to the unwilling passerby.

Meike warded off the water with their cloak, but some got on their shoes and cheek. They hopped to the side, avoiding a squirt of water from the oldest child. There was a shriek from behind them, and a mix of squeals from the fountain kids.

"Get out of there!" A tall woman brushed past Meike and charged at the kids, who scrambled off, hooting and sprinkling water into the air. "Ugh, I hate children," she said, turning back to Meike. "Oh, hello!" Her demeanor did a full shift, but that wasn't what had their tongue tied.

That spark of familiarity: goddess braids, the shells in her hair, and, for the first time since they'd woken up in this world, a skin tone similar to theirs. She was only a few years older, if they had to guess, somewhere in her mid-twenties.

"Are you..."

The woman smirked and held up a leather bag of her own. It was in better condition and had a stylized M on the front. "I've been studying under Madame Claudette since my sixteenth year."

"As an apprentice? I am, too. Sort of."

"I've never seen you before," she said. "Who do you work for?"

"Lady Griselda."

She frowned. "Sorry to hear that."

"Is that bad?"

"You're on the wrong side of town, my friend," she said. "What does an apprenticeship mean to you? What do you hope to gain?"

"Ideally, I'd like to learn how to make medicine. Potions and stuff. Maybe...a little magic?"

"You won't learn magic from her, I'm afraid. Griselda is a healer, not a mage." She placed a hand on her chest. "*I'm* studying magic, as well as alchemy and some minor herbalism. I was on my way to a client just now, actually."

'*Oh.*' Did this mean they'd have to start all over again? "But I already made a commitment..."

"Unfortunate. Madame Claudette isn't taking on any new apprentices at the moment, but I'm sure someone will have you."

"I don't know where to start. I'm new here."

She raised an eyebrow. "I can see that. Anyway, it was nice meeting you, but I need to get going."

"Wait! Um, what's your name? I'm Meike!"

"Moira. Wander around Sinnet enough, and you're sure to find like-minded individuals." And like that, she was off, leaving Meike alone and vulnerable to a surprise attack from the children.

"Brats," they said, but the child only laughed and darted away to cause more mayhem to a new target.

Meike found themself wishing it was possible to exchange numbers or had some idea of how to contact Moira in the future. Not that they even knew what to say, other than a timid greeting.

In their short time in this world, Meike became familiar with two major forms of communication: pigeon post and runners. And they were in no position to pay for either.

They made a promise to themself to pick up some proper jobs later, like shrooming, if it were still in demand. Worse case scenario, they find something in Anniken's field, or settle for some mind numbing busy work.

"Here you go..." They glanced up at the blue-eyed feline figure. It had blue black fur and wore a blue scarf around its neck. "You're Patches, right?"

The cat slowly blinked and nodded. Not the talkative type, but they could respect that. Patches extended a clawed hand, two silver pieces in its palm.

Meike took the money, and Patches plucked the packet of herbs from their hand. A little weird, but probably the best customer of the day.

6

A HARD PILL TO SWALLOW

"**I** did it," Meike said, holding out the empty bag for inspection. It was growing close to dinner, and they'd had nothing but stale bread and thin soup.

They were back in Griselda's shop, a shabby building when seen from the outside, but warm and lit by an array of candles lining the shelves and windows. And, beneath them, samples of her wares laid out on tables and shelves, mysterious bottles of potions and tea leaves. Meike longed to work within the store itself, assisting customers or mixing potions behind the counter.

"Took you all day, did it?" Griselda took the bag and searched the insides. "And the money?"

The coin purse they held onto. It wasn't much, but it was money well earned. And Griselda hadn't promised to pay them. "It's all here."

"Hand it over, then." She came at them like a vulture, and they stepped back to evade her itchy fingers.

"Do I have the job?" They recalled Pickles' swagger and tried to channel that into their tone.

"That remains to be seen," she said. "How do I know you didn't just dump everything in an alley and snatch that coin from elsewhere?" She tossed the bag aside. "Or that dog of yours, perhaps? I've seen him around, the little cut purse."

Meike held the bundle of coins close to their chest and pounding heart. They'd always heard that money could make people crazy, but never saw it firsthand. "Pickles showed me around, but he didn't do anything like that! Here, see for yourself."

Griselda snatched the bag from their hands and hurried to the counter, where she upended the contents and sorted through the coins. Meike was notoriously bad at math, but as they understood it, a hundred copper pieces equaled one silver, but the conversion of silver into gold eluded them. Mostly because they'd yet to be trusted with that amount of money, but gold seemed to be held in high esteem. People here scattered copper like they were pennies, but clung desperately to their gold.

"Everything seems to be in order," she said. She'd neatly stacked the silver and copper pieces into rows of five. "But if you're going to be here long term, I'm going to need you to demand that old woman hand over the big coin, and not these dirty little..." She tapped one of the copper stacks. "Silver, only. She knows how I feel about the small change. It's a chore converting it."

"Did I do good, then?"

"So it seems." She swept the silver coins into a separate bag, her own personal stash, a deep blue sprinkled with gold stars. "The copper is your pay. That's enough for two silver pieces, if you can find someone willing to take it."

Meike's eyes lit up. So they *were* being compensated! They returned the coins to the borrowed, beat up purse. It wasn't much, but it was theirs—enough for another night at the inn, and maybe something better than day old bread. "Thank you, Lady Griselda."

"You have to be firm," she said. "Tell the customers I only take silver and gold."

"Yes," they said. "I can do that. But does this mean I have a job?"

Griselda waved a hand in the air. "Oh, yes, why not? I'll still need to confirm some things, but I can make room for you. How does five silver a week sound?"

Five silver was the equivalent of five dollars, a few dollars short of the minimum wage of their home country. "I was hoping for a bit more..." Meike bit their lip. "Like a hundred silver?"

She let out a hooting laugh. "A *hundred*? Are you out of your mind, child? You should be lucky to get even one."

"But five silver isn't enough to live on!"

"Oh, dear." She gave them a sweet smile. "You may be a courier, but I don't fulfill orders on the daily."

"But..." They looked down at the bag in their hands, the pitiful collection of coins.

"Take another job," she said, like it was the simplest thing in the world. "There's always someone in need of your skills."

"I don't want to be a courier," they said. "I want to be like...I want to be like *you*."

"You'll have to look elsewhere, I'm afraid. I don't take on apprentices. I'm much too young for that!"

Meike sighed, the first of many, and placed the bag in their pocket. "Fine, then. I'll find someone who will."

"Go then," she said, turning her back to them. "I'll send for you when I need you."

"How? How do I know you won't forget, like last time?"

"I'll send my raven to find you."

They still had their doubts, but were growing tired and hungry, and Pickles had promised them food. "I'll keep an eye out for it," they said, and made their exit.

"Good evening, cats and kittens," Pickles said, full of vim and vigor. One didn't need to look under the table to spot his wildly wagging tail.

Meike mumbled a half-hearted greeting, and Anniken said nothing at all. Her hollow eyes and the bags beneath said it all: retail was taking its toll.

"...Tough crowd tonight," he said, and tucked his tongue back into his mouth.

"I had a long day," Meike said, and winced when their stomach growled in complaint.

They'd skipped lunch, and breakfast was so far away they were seeing double. And yet, they somehow had enough restraint to stave off impulse buying, a grand feat when you considered all the good food they passed along the way: savory soups, rolls fresh from the oven, rows and rows of produce, and an assortment of cheeses, from wheels of sharp cheddar to blocks sprinkled with nuts.

Two silver could go a long way, and Meike came close to buying just enough for a cheese and veggie sandwich.

"Bluh," Anniken said.

"Aptly put," Pickles said. "And how was the job, Mike? Find everything okay?"

They didn't have the strength to correct him. "She said she'd give me more work, but the pay is...it's pretty bad."

"Can't be worse than what I make," Anniken said. "Twenty silver a week is slave labor."

Meike's jaw dropped in dismay. "You're getting twenty?"

"You two are getting paid?"

"Not helping, dog," Anniken snapped. "I work at a clothing store that also offers tailoring. Decent stock, and the customers toss money around like it's nothing. When I'm not assisting customers, I'm patching up holes and fixing imperfections. I should be making two hundred, at the very least."

"Griselda offered me five…"

"Oh. Oh Meike, I'm so sorry." She gave them a pained expression, but Meike read no sincerity in her tone. It was more like pity.

"Five is nothing," Pickles said. "But twenty? You could afford a nicer room at the inn."

"That's nice and all, but I'd rather have my own apartment and toilet."

Meike lightly beat their knuckles on the table. "What about me? What am I going to do?"

"Get another job," Anniken and Pickles said in unison. She glared at him, and he sneered.

"She said the same thing…" The problem was they didn't want another job. They wanted just the one and to stay in their comfort zone.

"You're the plant nerd," Anniken said. "I'm sure you'll figure something out."

"That's what I thought before," they groaned, and laid their head on the table.

Meike told themself they could handle it, as long as they got to do something they loved. And what better place or time than this funky fantasy world? But they weren't counting on this, on dead-end jobs and menial tasks. Today they were a courier, tomorrow they could be scrubbing chamber pots by hand. Or gutting fish...

"Excuse me," a voice full of false cheer said somewhere above them.

Meike sat up and made room for their promised meal, and a bit more: two vegetarian strudels on a bed of shredded cabbage and carrots, and a hard roll on the side. Their drink was nothing glamorous; a glass of water and lemons on the side.

The server set down additional plates for the rest of their party: two steaks so rare they were practically dripping, and potatoes and meat for Anniken.

They squeezed lemon into their water while the server poured beer for the other two. Meike didn't understand the appeal; it tasted just as bad as the stuff back home and made Anniken uncharacteristically giddy. But it was the one thing she and Pickles could bond over.

"I'm not great at it," Anniken said, "But I can sew. If I practice at it, I could find an apprenticeship that way."

"You could," Pickles said, and tore into his steak, face first. It was too much to hope that a dog had table manners on par with a human. "Or you could find something worth doing. Didn't you say you studied the blade?"

"I said I took fencing classes, which isn't the same. Wasn't very good at it, either."

"Anyone can swing a sword, but having experience will make you stand out above a rookie who can't tell the difference between a cleaver and a hunting knife."

Meike nibbled on their lightly seasoned pastry. It was a small table, but the gap between them seemed large.

"Even if I could, what's the point? Can women become knights?"

"If you want to be a narc, sure." He licked his chops clean and held a paw in the air. "I'm thinking more small scale, and on your own terms."

"A bandit, then."

Pickles cocked his head to the side. "I can hook you up if you're interested, but I mean more in the terms of...monster hunting."

"Like quests," Meike blurted out. "I want to..." The word was on the tip of their tongue, but they lowered their head in shame. Pickles had his axe, Anniken could handle a blade, and Meike had...an unlimited knowledge of plants and fungi.

"You can help by studying under your boss and mixing potions," Pickles said. "But the battlefield is no place for an errand boy."

"I'm not..." They sighed. "You're going to want someone who can identify edible and poisonous plants, depending on how far you plan to go out. I may not know how to fight, but I'm still a valuable asset."

Pickles dunked his muzzle into his cup. Beer dripped from his fur when he came back for air, and Meike braced themself for the inevitable splatter. "You saying you know how to pacify a man-eating plant?"

"...That's not a thing, is it?" When Meike thought of man-eating plants, Audrey II or triffids came to mind, neither of which they hoped to encounter in real life.

He gave a brisk shake of his head, against the protests of the humans at the table. "Oh, you don't know the half of it, kid."

7

(Don't) Move Your Feet

The request board loomed over Meike, a mountain of chores, calls for action, and MLM schemes. They had a vague idea of what they wanted but probed the board for what Pickles mentioned previously: ventures far above their ability and pay grade.

The kobold quest was gone, but there were others in its place. Slaying quests targeting sewer rats the size of dogs, wild boars for their meat and hides, extermination of an exotic (and invasive) breed of bug, and many more. None that caught Meike's eye, and anyway, they'd be laughed off if they tried championing themself to the experts.

They sought smaller fish that spoke to their interests and expertise. Like the florist gig staring them right in the face. Meike held back a laugh; wasn't this what their mom wanted? Something simple, safe, and close to home?

Meike took the flyer, but also another catering to their love of fungi. A request similar to the one they found during their last job hunt—and from the same person, at that. "It's kismet," they said to themself.

Coprinellus micaceus, or Mica Cap. Assuming the buyer intended to consume them, young and fleshy was the way to go. Liquefied caps had no use as far as they knew, but people of this world may think differently.

The pay wasn't bad, either; six silver pieces per troop, five at the max. Thirty silver, and if they could wrangle it all in one day, that made it worth more than a month's pay from Griselda!

It almost sounded too good to be true, but it couldn't hurt to try.

They glanced at the florist job in their other hand and hastily stuffed it in their pocket. Now they just needed proper mushroom hunting gear. Meike jiggled their mostly empty coin purse and sighed. Moments like these required improvisation, and they once hunted morels with their dad's old hunting knife. Not the ideal tool; a proper morel knife needed a curve to avoid damaging the shroom and assist with debris removal.

With that in mind, they turned away from the board, plunged into the crowd, and ran right into someone. They gave a hasty apology and darted to the side.

"...Meike?"

They froze and slowly turned their head to look in the voice's direction. Very few people here knew their name, but they were delighted to see a familiar face. "Moira," they said, maybe a tad louder than desired, but nothing out of the ordinary for a high traffic area.

She gave them a polite nod. "Fancy seeing you here."

"Yeah! I mean, you too." A passerby behind gave Meike a hard shove to the side and kept going without apologizing.

Moira waved them out of the way of traffic. "Out on another job?"

"Sort of? I picked up some side jobs."

"Good thinking. I don't know what *she* pays, but Madame Claudette doesn't pamper me, either. Just enough to get by, but not live comfortably."

She surely got paid more than Griselda's five silver a week, but Meike didn't probe out of politeness.

"Well," they said, "I'm going shrooming. Mushroom hunting. It's worth thirty silver."

"Hm, thirty. How quaint." She held up her same bag from before. "I'm in the middle of potion delivery—my own stock."

"I think it's so cool that you make potions! That's what I'd rather be doing, but…"

"It's rather enjoyable, yes. But I'll spare you the details."

"I don't mind," Meike said. "I'd even be willing to take a class on it, if I could."

"You really should. Even a beginner could make respectable coin, if you work hard enough. There's a high demand from adventurers and travelers."

"Do you know anyone who could teach me?"

"Maybe, but you won't find that on the request board."

"I'm still finding my way around the city. Where's a good place to start?"

She gave them a curious look. "Academic circles, naturally."

"I've been meaning to get a new library card," they said, half-joking. But Moira wasn't picking up what they were putting down.

"You do that, then." She gave a low bow. "I'll see you when I see you, Meike."

And she was off again, leaving them alone to fight the crowd.

It would've been nice if she gave them actual directions, but Meike had nothing but time these days.

A basket was easy to come across. It was old, battered, and used to shuttle a pair of chickens, but clean and sturdy. Their owner would've gladly traded them for Meike's hoodie, but had to settle for their foreign and useless paper money—a crisp $5 bill.

A good knife was harder to find, as most being sold on the market were of quality design and intended for more nefarious uses. The cheaper knives went for ten silver, too rich for Meike's blood. But one silver, half a clutch of eggs, and ten ones passed off as a rare commodity, secured them a simple pocket knife.

It vaguely reminded them of a Bowie knife, albeit smaller, and with a serrated edge and wooden handle. It had a good weight to it, and the blade was wicked sharp.

"You're going to cut your hand off, kid," Pickles said, having taken the knife for inspection. He neatly slipped it into a test dummy.

"I'm not that clumsy." They'd gotten this far in life without broken bones or stitches, and knew to cut away from themself. "The only thing I plan on cutting are mushroom stalks and vegetation. And maybe some creepy crawlies."

"You'll find those for sure. Nothing major or even intelligent. But it might fuck up your night."

"If you're so worried, why don't you come with me? It'll go faster if I have protection, and dogs are natural mushroom hunters."

"What's in it for me," he said, side eying them, but his steadily wagging tail gave him away.

"I'll buy you a steak and give you a cut of the profits."

"Make it two, and I'm in."

It was a beautiful morning for mushroom hunting, but Meike was cooped up in a cramped storage room. The plan was to set out with Pickles before the crack of dawn, but Anniken scruffed them like a kitten, nearly choking Meike in the process and straining the stitching on their hood. Pickles smartly evaded her and hadn't been seen since.

"What gives," Meike said, massaging their poor neck. It was a simple black hoodie with the faded design of a Gundam, but it was one of the few clothes they'd brought along on this journey. And warmer than the cheap cloak Griselda loaned them.

"You aren't seriously going out in that, are you?" Anniken stood over them, fiddling with a rather rough looking shirt. It was like she cut out a pattern from a burlap sack.

"Did you make that?"

"It's a prototype," she said. "I need to do some measurements."

Meike swung their legs in the air, a show of defiance. She'd led them to this tiny room and forced them to sit on this very stiff table, and now she wanted to fit them for clothes?

"I'm going mushroom hunting, not preparing for a job interview."

"You're venturing into the wilderness with a dog. A dog that ditched us to sleep at the foot of that old crone's bed."

"That was..." Meike did some quick mental math. "Two weeks ago. I trust Pickles."

"I don't, which is why I want to make sure you're prepared." She stuffed them into the burlap sack. "I also need a practice doll, and you're the perfect model. I'd make a sweater for the dog too, but he always disappears on me."

"I wonder why," they said. It wouldn't be a bad thing to have more clothes, especially ones tailored to their surroundings. The less attention they drew to themself, the better—but not at the expense of their individuality! They resumed swinging their legs.

"Please hold still, or I'll prick you. On purpose," she added, as if she wasn't torturing them already.

It was a grueling two hours for Meike, who reluctantly played the role of dutiful doll, trying on a series of trousers, tunics, and a poncho that made them look like a walking billboard for a bee mixer—a goldenrod honeycomb pattern and a few black squares thrown into the mix. A fit they actually liked and were itching to showcase to the world. The only thing missing was a hood or cap.

Meike spun in a tight circle, trying in vain to produce a billowing effect.

"Please stand still," Anniken said, arms laden with fabrics in more subdued colors than Meike's current obsession. Blacks and browns, perfect for cutting a trail through the high grass or wading through muck.

"You know I can't afford any of this, right?"

"Obviously I'm buying it for you, just like I'm the one paying rent."

"Rent" was something like five or ten silver a week, in a leaky attic room. Anniken got the straw stuffed bed, and Meike had a little pallet on the floor. It was only a step above the cold cobblestones outside.

"I'll pay you back." Someday.

"Don't stress over it." She tossed hard leather pads at them. "Those go on your arms and legs."

Meike turned the leather guards over in their hands. Compared to the clothes, the "armor" was of lesser quality, rough and awkwardly slapped together. "I told you, Pickles will handle any monsters."

"Go and get your arms bitten off, for all I care," she said with a huff.

"Does this mean I can leave now?" Thanks to Anniken's interference, it was too late in the day to start the hunt, but they didn't want to hang around longer than necessary.

"Yes," she said, through tight lips.

"See you later, Annie," they said, and ran off, arms stretched out behind them and the back of their poncho floating.

"Psst. Hey, kid," a voice said outside of the shop. Pickles poked his head from around a barrel. "Is she gone?"

Meike jerked a thumb at the door. "She said she was making a sweater for you."

He crouched low to the ground and snarled. "If she comes at me with it, I'm taking the rest of her fingers. Nice digs, by the way." He batted at Meike's poncho. "Wouldn't mind having one of these..."

"You still can—" The flash of fangs made them reconsider. "I was thinking we could wait until tomorrow morning or tonight to go hunting. I need a break."

"Fine." He slumped onto his side, one ear comically flipped to the side. It was tempting to give him a belly rub. "Night is tricky. Let's leave it for tomorrow, yeah?" He narrowed his eyes. "And don't let her catch you."

Easier said than done.

8

Don't Feed the Plants

"It really is a nice poncho," Pickles said, trotting at Meike's heels. "Gotta get me one of those, but from someone respectable."

"Anniken did a great job on this." They tugged at the front of their poncho. It was thick and warm, presumably made from wool. Other than a few flaws here and there, it was an immaculate piece. Meike wished they could say the same about the pants and tunic, but they had a hard time sitting still for their fitting.

"Maybe I was wrong about her. If she keeps at it, she could be a decent tailor in the future. That's an easier job than fightin'."

It was early enough that the sun had yet to make an appearance. Calm, peaceful, and for a moment, Meike truly felt alone in the world.

"I don't think she wanted me to leave the city. She's worried I'll get hurt." There was something about her lately that they just couldn't quite place.

"You're safe with me," he said, turning off the main road onto a dirt path.

Meike followed along and tried to make themself as small as possible to avoid snagging their clothes on the crisscrossing branches. The dense path opened up to a sloping hill, with more on the horizon.

Before them stretched a playground of fallen logs, blankets of moss, tall grass, and briar patches. No sign of monsters, only bunnies, birds, and deer.

"There we are," he said, jaw widening for a yawn. "Even you can handle the meadows." Clark Meadows, according to the shoddy wooden sign on the road.

"You said there were man-eating plants. What do they look like?"

"Oh right, you've never seen one, have you? That flower field you came from is full of them!"

"Like Rafflesia?" They recalled nothing out of the ordinary, aside from Anniken being buried underground.

"Is that what you call them? But no, these are different." He sat back and shaded his eyes. "They come up with the sun, but are sluggish until noon. Easy to outrun in that state. You just can't get too close to them—there, there's one!" He pointed at an object near a cluster of trees.

Meike squinted at it, but it just looked like a tree to their uncultured eyes. "It doesn't look like anything to me."

"I'd draw you a picture, but I like the more hands on approach."

In hindsight, it might've been best to do research at a library, but Meike still needed to *find* one. "I'll just be extra careful."

Once at the bottom of the hill, Meike retrieved the knife from their basket and held it at the ready. It was far less impressive than Pickles' axe, but sharp enough to deal with a gluttonous plant.

"We're looking for Mica caps," they said.

"*You're* looking for caps. I'm just the muscle."

"They're very recognizable," Meike continued, ignoring him. "They usually grow around rotted trees and are light orange. But there's also look-alikes that can be poisonous, so you need to know the difference between the two."

He let out a loud yawn. "Are they the funky little bell shaped ones?"

"Yes. They're very common, which is why I'm so confident. I'll teach you how to identify them."

It was Pickles' turn to follow, leaving Meike to plunge deeper into the undergrowth. It was nice, being outside the city and inhaling fresh air—far fresher than anything they were used to back home. Meike attributed that to the lack of technological influence and pollution.

They kept their eyes low, scanning the ground and tree trunks.

"Found one," Pickles said, from a few feet away. He braced his front paws against a log, and with one great push, rolled it over.

Ants, worms, and other creepy crawlies came tumbling out of the rotten wood. Meike almost mistook the cluster of pale lavender bulbs for grub worms. A few more leaked onto the ground at Pickles' feet.

Meike crouched beside him and gently brushed a trail of ants away from one of the bigger bulbs.

"*Coprinus comatus*, or Shaggy Mane. These are still babies." Meike had no use for them, but it would be a waste to pluck the juveniles. "They look like tiny, inky umbrellas when they mature. Not my favorite, but I'll try to keep an eye on them."

Pickles snapped and devoured a few of the ants and one wiggly boy. "But can you eat them?"

"Only if you're brave enough."

"I'm plenty brave."

Meike didn't doubt that, but also couldn't remember if Shaggy Mane made you loopy like Inky caps. They hadn't counted on ending up here, otherwise they would've held tight to their foraging guide.

"I like your instincts, but remember that I'm looking for Mica caps, little orange mushrooms that grow in clusters."

"Orange bells, orange bells," he mumbled to himself, nose close to the ground. "What about these," he said a moment later, ears and tail perked and looking very much like a "good boy."

They glanced at the cluster and did a double take. It resembled *Cantharellus cibarius*, but that orange hue was the key difference between real and false Chanterelle. "Not even close to Mica." They poked the sunken innards of one mushroom. "These are shaped more like cups than bells. They're *Hygrophoropsis aurantiaca*."

"But it's orange and grows together," he said.

"There are a lot of mushrooms that fit that description, like the poisonous um...we call them carved pumpkins where I come from, but they're big and floppy and sometimes resemble Chanterelle."

"Why don't you take the lead then, smartass?" He plopped down on the fakes and stared at them.

"But that's what I've been trying to do from the start! If you'd stop running ahead and let me work—" Something warm, fleshy, and sticky brushed Meike's cheek and landed on their shoulder. The weight of it almost sent them to their knees, and the stench of rotten meat and sickly sweet nectar clogged their sinuses.

"Don't move," Pickles said, ears pulled back. He reached back with restrained movements, and pulled his axe free.

Meike couldn't move, even if they wanted to. Both the mounting dread and horror, accompanied by their instinct to flee, would not allow them to. "Hurry," they squeaked.

"That's a man-eating plant." His lips barely moved as he spoke, eyes leveled at the thing behind them.

Fortunately for them, the plant was slow, but the series of furry tentacles encircling Meike's body were uncomfortably tight. Worse yet were the secretions and the sensation of their skin baking beneath the poncho. Anniken would not be happy if they came back with her handiwork in tatters.

'At least I'll die doing what I loved.' And going back to the earth, to feed the worms, deer, and sprout new trees and fungi, if they're lucky.

"Stop crying," a voice on their side of the white tunnel snapped. "It just makes you tastier."

Meike yipped and took an involuntary step backwards, deeper into the creature binding them. There was another solid whack, closer to their hands.

"You have a knife! Use it!" Another whack near their shins sent them toppling forward, and if not for the stubborn plant, would've fallen flat on their face.

One downside to their majestic poncho was how much the fabric got in the way. There was no way to cut themself free without catching it on their blade—"Oh," Meike said, and let their body go limp. It wasn't the perfect escape, but if they wiggled just so...

The poncho slid over their shoulders and briefly caught on their neck, but Meike wrested their head free and slumped onto the ground. Pickles danced nimbly around their head, battling the poncho dressed plant and probably tearing both to shreds, but hey, they were alive.

Meike scrambled for their knife, dropped during the initial assault and laying forgotten with their basket. They took one glance at the scuffle behind them and decided they wanted to keep on living, and took refuge in a clump of bushes. It wasn't a triffid or an Audrey II, or even a Rafflesia, but a monstrous construct best described as a Sundew on steroids.

"Hi-yah! Meike, where are you? It's just one plant, we can take it!"

"I'm fine," they said in a loud whisper. "It sounds like you've got it under control."

"Are you kidding me?"

The ground shook and Pickles let out a yelp and a series of whimpers. Meike tentatively rolled to face the slaughter and peeked through their fingers.

The plant lay sprawled on the ground, much of its tentacles hacked off and a sluggish red sap oozing from its corpse. Next to it was Pickles, rubbing furiously at his ears.

Meike crawled out of their hidey hole, eying the plant with caution. If this were a horror movie, it would give one final jump scare before keeling over for good. "Is it dead?"

"No thanks to you," he snarled. "What *was* that?"

"You said you'd protect me!"

"Yeah, but that was before you up and left me." He spat on the tentacle trapped beneath his paw. "It's only an over-sized weed, but I would've been in trouble if it brought friends."

"Are you...are you hurt?"

He pawed at his ears. "No, it's just loud."

Meike kicked a tentacle away from their poncho, which was only mildly ruined. "Sorry," they mumbled, and wiggled back into it. "I got scared."

"The White One's annoying, but I reckon she would've stayed."

"You aren't going to tell her, are you?"

"Is that what you're worried about?" He sighed and massaged his forehead. "Try not to get caught again. Cause next time I might leave you."

Maybe tangling with plants and other horrid creatures was an everyday occurrence for *him*; the speed at which things progressed certainly made it seem so. But Meike, who didn't know how to throw a punch, let along wield a knife, found the whole experience deeply unsettling.

How quickly things returned to normal! The birds were back to singing, bunnies frolicking, and lazy bumblebees drifted through the air.

"*Tremella mesenterica*, witches butter," they said to themself. It was still in the jelly stage, mostly yellow with hints of orange. Once it solidified, the orange would take over, sometimes turning a dark red. It was fun to poke and read about, but had little to offer beyond that.

Pickles stuck his nose into it and gave the little parasite a curious lick. "Eh, I like the shanties better. They smelled pretty nice."

"Chanterelle." The plants might not kill him, but their non-sentient cousins might. "Anyway, I've found them." They pointed their knife at the cluster of Mica caps at the base of the tree. A healthy and mature crowd. "Please don't," they said, just as Pickles lowered his head and opened his jaw, just mere seconds from snapping up a handsome specimen.

"Fine," he snapped, and returned to standing guard while Meike worked.

The caps were grouped together in a defensive pattern, and took some time to extract, but the additional weight to their basket was uplifting. Soon, their little shroom friends would spread their spores across the meadow, a trail of microscopic breadcrumbs.

"First batch done!" They held the basket in triumph.

"Oi, what do you mean 'first'?"

"I didn't come all the way out here for a few caps," they said. "The basket needs to be full."

"Add some of those puff balls or shanties we found. They won't know the difference."

"I think the client can tell the difference between a Mica cap and a Chanterelle, Pickles." They lightly rattled the basket. "Come on, I'm sure there's more nearby. It's like how they say 'where there's smoke, there's fire!'"

"No one says that," he said, but plodded after them. "I hope it's worth almost dying for."

9

WHY BE A WALLFLOWER?

They were exhausted by the end, but the heft of Meike's basket was all that mattered. Next to the safety of vital organs, of course. Pickles spotted and dispatched of several more of the monstrous plants, while Meike hung back, pitiful knife in hand.

It seemed inevitable, as the plants worked together on a frequency Meike and Pickles lacked access to, and lurked near the choice mushrooms.

"They're really persistent, huh," Meike said, once the worst of it was behind them. Other than the Mica caps, they managed to salvage a *Sparassis*—cauliflower mushroom!—while Pickles distracted a plant. A little treat for all their hard work, and dinner for tonight.

"That's one way to put it," he said, slinging the axe over his back. "But look, kid. You're gonna have to learn to fend for yourself. My back hurts from all this carrying."

"I will. Once I learn a little magic." Meike pointed a finger into the air and imagined a spark of flame lingering on their fingertip. Spirit gun!

"Have you looked into that yet? Laeford's great, but there's more to Glasend than that. I've been all over, and it's not even my favorite city."

"I know, but I hate moving around so much. And Laeford has everything I need and want." It also offered familiarity and stability. It would be harder finding work if they were constantly on the move.

He cocked his head at them. "You're young. Don't worry about settling until your forties."

Forties...that was almost twenty years away, and difficult to grasp. They hoped to be back home long before then, or at least of better standing in their current station. "I guess it wouldn't be a bad idea to be prepared when I have to travel. I wanna be able to zap bandits if they try to ambush me."

"Ambitious, but you should stick with the basics first. That knife of yours isn't made for combat, but it'll do for now. Use the money from your shrooms to buy a cheap sword. Something light."

"But I'm saving up for magic lessons, and food, and..." Meike sighed and ran a hand through their hair. Ideally, they'd like to afford their own room at the inn, with an actual apartment being the distant and nigh impossible dream. No matter where they went, money seemed to run their life.

"Sword first." He let out a loud yawn. "Once you start huntin', the money will roll in."

"I keep telling you I'm a vegetarian. I don't eat meat, and I don't want to kill defenseless animals."

"They aren't 'defenseless'. A bunny nearly gutted one of my old playmates. He got it on its back and..." He made a sort of hissing sound in the back of his throat and drew a paw along his belly. "Boars and deer will gladly run you down. Everything wants to kill you, even the squirrels."

"Oh, come on. Squirrels are weenies." Besides, it would take an entire herd to take down one human, and while Meike would admit to being weak, they would not allow themself to be bullied by rodents.

"We'll start small for you. Young boars or bunnies, if that's too much."

"I don't know about this..." But knew they'd get dragged along somehow. Meike tried to tell themself the meat and hides would be put to good use; it'd be a waste otherwise. But the thought of putting sword to flesh made them queasy.

Pickles stamped his paws on the familiar cobblestone of Laeford, like a child eager to get snow off the bottoms of their boots. "I'm going to nap. Don't forget you promised to feed me, cause I won't," he growled, and sauntered off.

"How could I..." Meike glanced down at their grimy attire. It wasn't entirely trashed, but it could definitely use a wash. But they could worry about that later.

Now that they were better familiar with the city, tracking down the requester took them less than an hour—and out to an area of the city they'd only caught glimpses of so far, but had no real reason to explore.

Partly because of the gated community vibes, and the very literal gates, topped with spikes to discourage people from scaling them to vine choked red bricked buildings and lush gardens beyond.

Meike gripped the bars between their hands and poked their head in. There was a courtyard with marble benches, carefully trimmed hedges, beds of gorgeous roses in reds, blues, and blacks—

"Excuse you," one half of a couple cuddled up on a bench said. "Do you mind?" He'd been in the middle of exchanging saliva with his partner, which Meike found distasteful in any situation.

"I was admiring the plants," they said. *'Not you.'*

"Please go away." He made a shooing gesture, and if he were a lot closer, Meike might've taken a page out of Pickles' book and bitten him.

"I'm also here on business." They held up the basket. "Mushroom delivery. Can you let me in?"

The man mouthed "No," but his partner abandoned him to unlock the gate. "You must be here to see Maggie. She's a bit of a mushroom fanatic."

"Me too!" They wiggled through the gate before she could change her mind, and forced themself to take slower and constrained steps. It was all too tempting to run at full speed down the narrow and newly cobbled street, but that and their filthy cloak would only draw unwanted attention.

Maggie's house stood out from the cookie cutter mold: several tacky mushroom statues, toadstools, and dwarves littered her front lawn. Meike's kind of person.

They skipped up the front steps and rapped on the door, expecting a mousy-haired woman with kind eyes and cradling an over-sized rat or log. A sweet, if odd, older woman willing to take them under her wing and possibly offer long term or permanent employment.

What they got instead almost caused Meike to turn and run—if their feet weren't firmly rooted to the ground, mind set on finishing their quest and beginning a new chain for their ultimate goal.

The red, gaping mouth of a Venus flytrap greeted them at the door, and inquired in a soft voice, "Can I help you, dear?"

"It's been so long since I last had anyone over," Maggie said, having sat Meike down for tea. Now that they had an opportunity to see her in a more neutral lighting, she was actually rather pretty. Once you looked past the spiky "teeth", lack of visible eyes, and dark green skin.

Her house was far more mundane than they expected, the kind only a grandmother could love. Doilies and tiny glass figurines lined every surface, and common house plants stood guard in the corners and windows. But she had a pet toad in a large glass tank on one wall, and a shy cat who occasionally poked a paw out to bat at Meike's poncho or shoe laces.

Meike sipped at their dandelion tea. It was certainly...different from what they were used to. They were familiar with the benefits of dandelions; it was a natural source of iron and vitamin C, for one. But it was also bitter, and not even milk and sugar could make up for it.

"Been a while for me, too." A lifelong affair, really. Their childhood was terribly lonely, and friends were difficult to come by. If they wanted camaraderie and inclusion, they turned to video games and books, where they were free to be anyone and go on epic adventures. For Meike, loneliness, and hell, was other people, particularly those quick to point out their quirks and actively work to exclude them.

"I used to be quite the social butterfly," Maggie said, and tilted her head back. The tea cup briefly disappeared into her "trap," where the sound of gulping could be heard from her throat. Aside from her head, the rest of her body was mostly human. Large, fan-like leaves flanked her sides, and vines grew from the top of her tunic to the tips of her toes.

"What happened?"

"You're looking at it," she said, and took another "sip".

"I was wondering about that!" They slapped their hands on their knees and leaned forward. "How did you..."

"Magic."

"I figured that, but I mean, what *kind* of magic? Are you a witch? Or is mage the better term?" The world needed to know! *Meike* needed to know.

Maggie laughed at a frequency Meike only barely registered. The quality was something akin to reeds rubbing together, punctuated by soft bird calls.

"My human form was limiting and not at all how I perceived myself. So I became one with nature, a feat achieved with the aid of a high-ranking alchemist." She placed the cup in her mouth and crushed it. "I like the term witch for myself, but I'm really a better herbalist than a spellcaster, I'm afraid to say."

Meike's hand shot into the air. "We're the same! Sort of, anyway. I, too, find my flesh prison limiting."

"Oh, that's nice, dear, but I'm afraid I can't help you. They designed the potion with my body type in mind."

"'It's my hole, it was made for me,'" they said, a reference only they understood, but Maggie chuckled along as if she were in on the joke.

"If you're interested, I could give you the name of the alchemist I worked with."

"I appreciate it, but I can't really afford that right now." Nor were they keen on the idea of morphing their body into a tree person. "My skill level isn't high for it, either. I'm more of a...novice, you could say."

"Ah. Is that why you're still chasing quests from the board? I am glad for the caps, don't get me wrong. But mushroom hunting is more a hobby than a true profession. It simply doesn't pay much."

"I'm starting to realize that, yes." They curiously nibbled on the rim of their cup, and while there was a firmness on the surface level, applied pressure caused it to chip beneath their teeth. It tasted of toasted petals, a not entirely unpleasant flavor. "I was actually hoping I could work under you. But now I'm wondering if you take on apprentices?"

"For the right student, perhaps. But I can't offer you room and board, and apprentices rarely get paid by their masters."

"Oh..." At least they could say they tried, but hearing "no" all the time was growing old.

"Might I propose something beneficial for the both of us?"

Meike perked up, the string of hope so close they could reach out and grasp it. "I have a knack for identifying plants!"

"That's part of it. I'm getting on in my age, and can't risk venturing out into the woods these days. The rabbits have grown bold."

"My friend said they're brutal. Is it really that bad?"

"For weaklings, such as me. But you're young, healthy, and came out unscathed."

"I'm one tough cookie," they said. Maggie didn't need to know the gritty details. "I can handle a few bunnies!"

"Excellent news. So, I'll teach you everything I know, if you forage for me. Herbs, mushrooms, insects. I'll even supply the materials, at least in the beginning. Once you're at a satisfactory level, you'll have to provide for yourself."

"I can do that. I have a knack for identifying plants." And so far, they'd only seen a handful of plants they couldn't put a name to. Insects were trickier, but that's what libraries were for. But oh, what wonderful news! It wouldn't be done behind a screen or with fun mini-games, but an actual mortar and pestle, and maybe even a cauldron!

"I'd also like a few plump rabbits. Alive if possible, but dead, skinned, and deboned works just as well. Twice a week is ideal, but if you can bring more..."

Meike snapped out of their potion crafting daydreams and leaned back in their seat, tea forgotten. Maggie's cat took this as an invitation to pounce on their foot and bat their laces around like it was hyped up on catnip.

"You want me to...kill?"

"Of course." She stroked the bottom half of her mouth, lingering on the tips of her teeth. "I *am* a carnivorous plant, after all."

"You're quiet," Anniken said, peering at them over her copy of the *Daily Crawler*, a newspaper strictly about questing and the usual monsters one would encounter in the wild. She'd recently acquired a sword, something cheap and simple, but sharp enough to slap a few pigs around.

"I'm exhausted," Meike said. They had two jobs now; one that paid peanuts, the other that paid in experience. And Maggie was pushing for those rabbits. It was really looking like she'd made a deal with Pickles behind their back.

"Same." Based on the light accumulation of muscle and the bandages on her hands and forearms, her definition of exhaustion was clearly out of their league. "Fencing never prepared me for this level of sparring. The swords we use aren't technically even weapons."

"Does Pickles know that?"

There was a devious twinkle in her eye. "Doesn't need to. It's really not that bad once you get into the swing."

Meike rubbed their arm, laced with superficial cuts from foliage and the occasional scuffle with a territorial rabbit. "I still need a sword."

"I can give you this one when I upgrade, probably by the end of the week."

They gave an unenthusiastic "Yay."

"Don't give me that. Pickles told me how you ran from an over-sized houseplant. You're going to need to defend yourself if you want to keep leaving the city walls."

"I'm...a fast runner," they said. "And I know how to avoid monsters."

"That's not good enough." She narrowed their eyes at them, and Meike wanted to crawl into their tiny pallet and disappear. "Do you know what I find interesting, Meike?"

"...Is that a rhetorical question?"

"This place seems oddly relevant to *your* interests. Like it was made for you."

"You mean like my own personal heaven?" Glasend was nice and all, but it lacked a steady internet connection.

"If you want to go with the theory that we both died that day, sure." But then, what happened to the other people on the train? Why would it just be the two of them? "Could still be purgatory. Or..."

"Meike, if you say video games or anime, I'm going to smack you." Her head disappeared behind the paper. "There are no menus, and items don't fast craft at the push of a button."

'Dang.' But then why were there lizard people and talking dogs? That part they didn't understand. "Maybe it is purgatory, and we're stuck in some alternate timeline." That would explain the similarities between this world and their own.

"Where everything went to shit, apparently. And we're stuck in the Florida of the Midwest, Ohio."

"Ohio isn't *that* bad. Cleveland's pretty good, at least. Balto, the Rock n Roll Hall of Fame, metroparks..."

"Cleveland? One of the gloomiest cities in the country? And then there's the toxic river that's literally caught on *fire*."

"You got me there," they said. "But if we're willing to consider alternate timelines...what about dreams?"

"Well, that settles that," she said, and folded her newspaper. "If we're in your dream, maybe the solution is as easy as killing you. That's certain to wake you up."

Meike didn't like the casual tone in her voice, or that the sword was now in her lap and partially unsheathed.

"I'm joking," she said, seeing the look on their face. "But the dream theory seems unlikely, unless we're both sharing dreams, and I don't believe in that nonsense."

"Right," they said, and tried to force a laugh. Meike had enough money to rent their own room for the night; foraging for Maggie allowed them to pick up a few things for themself along the way. So while it wasn't a grand feast, food wasn't too big an issue these days.

"What we should be doing is looking for the people who rode in with us. Maybe they'd have a better clue of what's going on."

"Anniken, this sounds like a quest."

"Don't do that," she said, waving a finger at them. "It's not a quest. We're just trying to get some answers."

Meike swallowed the urge to call it a mystery. They didn't know how fast she was with that blade, but didn't want to tempt her, either.

"And we won't get that by staying here."

"But Laeford is safe," they blurted out. It was big, relatively safe, and full of resources. It wasn't a capital city, but close to it. "You can leave if you want, but I'm staying."

"Finally standing up for yourself, I see." She sighed and sheathed the sword. "I will not become an isekai title..." Her eyes darted away from theirs. "'I Died And Was Reborn As A Retail Worker.' Probably been done, but it's accurate. And I hate it."

"But what else are you going to do for money?"

"I'll do what Pickles does, but not banditry. I have more respect for myself than that."

Meike glanced at their poncho, all patched up and ready for tomorrow's misadventures. "You're an excellent seamstress. You don't have to fight."

"I am, but I lack passion to see it through like you. I crave adventure, even if kills me."

She fell silent, and after a few minutes of that, returned to her reading. Meike slumped onto their pitiful bed. This was it—after this week or sometime after, the party was splitting. Question was, would Anniken leave on her own, or take Pickles with her?

10

DIGESTIVE HEALTH

Most of what Meike knew about rabbits came from a book—Watership Down, where the bunnies had human characteristics and loved a good bedtime story. They couldn't count beyond four and were all named after plants, or the Lapine language, if they were female and wild. It was one of their favorite books, but dwelling on it now only reminded them of all they'd lost.

Meike sighed and shifted in their spot in the tall grass. Fiction aside, there were more concrete facts about rabbits. Such as their waking and sleeping hours. Like hamsters and guinea pigs, they were crepuscular, and ventured out of their burrows and scrapes around dusk and dawn each day, without fail. But unlike rodents, rabbits relied on their powerful hind legs to defend themself, and while it was cute from afar, hit hard with their tiny rabbit fists. Meike witnessed the latter firsthand, having seen Pickles play fight with one before snapping its neck.

"Be on the ready," Pickles said, mouth subtly twitching in the dark. He hugged his belly low to the ground, tail end perked in preparation for the hunt.

Today would not be like the last, when they got bullied by several bucks almost the size of their corgi mentor. Pickles took out two of them, and Meike accidentally kicked one before trapping it under their foot. At least until it got its claws into their shins. Anniken's cheap leg guards came in handy that day, but Meike didn't make it out without a scratch.

'I bet she has some pretty cool gear now,' they thought, eyes trained on the base of a hollow tree.

It wasn't just the sword Anniken invested in, but a full set of armor. Nothing heavy like chain or plate mail, but something light to move in, like leather. They'd seen so little of her as of late, but the small group occasionally sat for meals. And it was there Meike learned about the armor, picking at their bowl of assorted beans and rice while Pickles happily engaged her.

The tip of a curious nose appeared from the burrow hidden beneath the tree. Pickles tensed up and crawled forward a step. Meike followed, taking care to muffle their clumsier movements. One wrong move and the game was lost.

The nose quickly vanished into its hole, and both Pickles and Meike held their breath while they awaited its return.

It returned almost a full minute later, extending its head from the hole, making quick glances from side to side, and freezing on the space between Meike and Pickles. And then it hopped forwards and upwards, clearing a low-hanging branch and bush like it expected snares. But these rabbits were smarter than the ones Meike knew of back home.

It made a few cautious hops as it put further distance between it and the safety of its home, hindquarters twitching for the dash into the clearing. It was a large buck, all black but for the streak of white on its tail. A worthy opponent for Pickles, who darted out of the brush and came snapping and snarling.

The rabbit stood its ground and raised up on its hind legs, a paw soaring for and narrowly missing the corgi's head. Pickles crashed into it and sent it sprawling and leaping, and pounced squarely on its back before it could slip away.

"Look at the fight in this one," he hollered back to Meike, who stood back with the knife dangling by their side.

"He's almost too pretty to kill," Meike said. It was a shame they couldn't be friends, but Maggie had to eat.

"Don't talk nonsense," he growled, teeth buried deep into the rabbit's neck. It thrashed and screamed and Meike could do nothing but turn their head. Watching the killing of a living creature was too much for their delicate constitution.

Pickles opened his jaw and out plopped the rabbit, looking far less handsome in its eternal sleep. It was only going to get worse from here, and Meike wanted to bolt and leave the rabbit's slayer to the task.

"Okay, grab him and we'll go out by the river."

The locals called it the Dividing River. Meike didn't like getting too close to it. It seemed calm and peaceful from afar, but stand close enough and the current churned and rushed and threatened to swallow you up. That, or the gators would suck you in.

"I don't wanna," they whined, but did as told. It was horrible work, gutting and skinning a rabbit, but someone had to do it. And that someone was the poor unfortunate soul half hiding the rabbit under their poncho, to shield the crime from the other woodland creatures, but mostly to avoid its accusatory gaze.

"Lay it on its back," he said, sitting at the edge of the river. "Get it all nice and neat."

"Please don't make this harder than it already is," Meike said, and crouched low to the ground. They splayed the rabbit out and neatly rearranged its limbs. It was still warm to the touch.

"Now." He leaned forward. "Slit it from top to bottom."

"I know that much." It thankfully went pretty well; having a sharp knife and a skilled hand was the deciding factor. All those biology classes had some use after all, but they didn't teach you how to skin an animal. It was arguably their least favorite part of the process, as it required some force to unclothe the rabbit.

Pickles claimed the skin as his reward for slaying the creature. Once Meike felt comfortable with the process, they could turn in the hides themself. Rabbits weren't much on their own, but kill enough and you could make a tidy profit. Or so Pickles claimed.

"One thing...how do I debone this?"

"I could do it for you," he said. "At a—"

"Price, I know." They sighed and cleaned the blood off their hands. "I'd do it myself, but I don't want to ruin it."

"Does it have to be deboned?"

It technically didn't have to be killed, but they hated the idea of the poor things being digested alive. "I guess she won't complain too much..."

"Don't throw away the innards," he said, licking his chops. "I want that little heart and liver."

"Gross!" They collected the skinned rabbit and moved aside to allow the dog his prize. He ate up the raw bits, looking quite pleased with himself.

"Good stuff. You're missing out."

"I'll pass, thanks." Now to get this to Maggie before it spoiled. Meike could only hope she didn't develop a craving for boars.

"What a marvelous specimen," Maggie said, having slurped up the last of the rabbit.

Meike tried not to stick around to watch her eat. It wasn't a fast process; the meat lingered in her "mouth," the way it did in a snake's stomach. Very on brand for a carnivorous plant, and she only needed to be "fed" every few days.

"You'd save a lot of time and trouble if you brought me a live bun or two. I like them...fresh." She "smiled," all teeth and scant previews of her most recent meal.

"It's not that simple, or I would," they said, desperately trying to not imagine the poor thing squirming and shrieking to be free. "Also, wouldn't that hurt you? Having to eat a live rabbit?"

"Oh, don't worry about me," she said, ignoring the lump of flesh. That was another thing about her condition; speaking didn't require her "lips" to flap. It was like talking directly to a phone speaker. "Once the prey is trapped, it has no means of struggle. But also, I like to give them a hard little knock on the head. By the time they come through, my digestive enzymes and constriction—"

"I'm good, thanks." Meike averted their eyes away from Maggie. No way. They tolerated the bunny slaying, but would never allow her to devour one alive. They lost many a night from the nightmares surrounding Maggie's eating habits. "Can we focus on potion craft today?"

"Of course, dear." She dabbed her mouth with a fancy cloth napkin with her initials etched in a pale blue: MS. Maggie Sinclair. A perfectly normal name for a perfectly normal woman.

"Grab your things and come along."

Meike followed her into the kitchen and glanced around at the cozy room. A magenta kettle rested on the stovetop, dried herbs, braided garlic, and fish dangled from the ceiling...it had a very modern but rustic look to it. The oven and fridge were out of sync with the world outside, but Meike chalked that up to the wealthy neighborhood. Until now, the only areas available to them were decidedly "lower class."

"We're working here?" Not that they minded. The kitchen table was big enough for four people and made from nice, sturdy wood, and so well polished it might as well have been brand new. There were only two chairs, but one could argue that Maggie's appearance was a passive means of discouraging company. Meike naturally assumed the extra chair was for them.

"Oh, no." She cleaned off the kitchen counter. "My workroom is downstairs." And before Meike could question further, she reached under the counter and swung it upwards. There'd been a simple purple curtain beneath, which they'd assumed was to hide her pots and pans.

But there was no cast iron skillet or dutch oven. Just a series of stairs descending into darkness.

"Um."

Maggie's cat streaked past them and into the darkness below. "I don't work as much as I used to, so I'm afraid it's not properly lit. Here." She held up a finger, and a small ball of light manifested.

"Spirit gun," they whispered, awed by the glowing light, now independent of Maggie's direct influence. It drifted down the stairs, a shorter flight than they feared. Waiting for them on the landing was the cat.

The workroom was far less cozy than the rest of her house (what little they'd seen of it, so far). It was very Spartan, sacrificing aesthetics for practicality. There was an old wooden cabinet, two tables, one lined with a variety of jars, mysterious liquids, crawling insects, and...

Meike made a face and focused more on the adjacent table, empty but for the mortar and pestle and cutting board. The lack of windows concerned them; how did she filter fumes? But it was quiet and free from distraction.

They were finally going to explore healing magic! Not that they needed to leave Earth to do that, but potions and salves were standard care in this world.

"But where's the uh..." Cauldron danced on the tip of their tongue, but that sounded so cliche. "How do we cook this?"

"Right, I forget you aren't magically inclined..."

"Yet."

Maggie fetched them a small pot and box. She stacked them together and placed a shard of pink glass into the groove of the box.

"What does that do?"

"It's a lighter. You crack it against the table and toss into the little burner here." She fell silent for a second, head cocked back as she patted her chest. "Sorry, digestion issues. But this is called a *mana shard*. It makes *fire*."

"I figured as much," they said, scowling in return. This was, Meike was learning, the downside to working for eccentric rich people.

"Good." She rubbed her belly. "I'll be upstairs if you need me."

She'd gone over the basics with them earlier. If you broke it down in simple terms—chop, grind, boil, and store—the process was deceptively easy. More advanced potions required extra steps or a bit of magic.

They glanced down at their instruments and the lone hand of ginger. Meike's bag was filled with other mundane plants, like turmeric, *chamomile*, and lavender. Easy to come across, but most accessible from the local market, with foreign vendors carrying plants more than twice what Meike made in a week, and completely unrecognizable to their uncultured eyes. *Those* had to have a touch of magic to them, or at least a taste you couldn't find anywhere else.

Meike neatly chopped the ginger bit by bit, focusing on the finger-like protrusions until they worked their way to the base. It was easier and more pleasant than dissecting a rabbit, and almost just as messy. They wondered if it wouldn't be better to simply grate the whole thing. Annoying, yes, but a better use for the natural yeast in the root. That's how it worked for ginger beer, when it was still in the tea stage.

They added the ginger and water to the pot and picked up the odd shard. For a fire starting tool, it was rather cold. They gave it the lightest of taps before banging it down on the table. Heat rose to Meike's fingertips, and they quickly dashed it into the burner before it went off.

But there was no grand explosion, or even a tremor. The stone simply expanded into a blocky flame. It was actually kind of cute once they calmed down from the initial shock.

Meanwhile, the water in the pot came to an abrupt simmer, and a rolling boil past the thirty second mark. It was a shame they didn't have their phone to document the entire process for the rest of the gang. This stuff was probably nothing new to Pickles, but Anniken would surely take some interest.

They swirled the contents around with a long, thin spoon. Maggie didn't give them an exact time, just a vague, "You'll know when you see it." Five minutes was long enough for Meike, who first tried blowing on the magical flame to extinguish it. It burned brighter in defiance, and with no other option, they carefully separated the pot from the burner and set it down on the heavy table.

Leaving the pot to cool, they made another attempt to snuff out the flame. This time, by suffocation. They placed a jar over it and watched the flame squirm and retreat to the base, flattening itself along the surface to soak up whatever oxygen remained. It was still hanging on when Maggie came down some twenty minutes later.

"You did a good job," she said, taking the bottle of unsweetened ginger tea. She sniffed it, and pleased by the results, tipped the lukewarm liquid into her mouth. "Very good. Just needs a little sugar and lemon."

Meike tapped the jar of trapped fire. "About this."

"That's nothing." She made a flapping motion with her hand, and the flame disappeared. "I'm going back upstairs to settle my stomach. Prepare more of the tea, and while that's cooling, get started on the burn cream. You'll find more shards in the cabinet." And like that, she was off. Only her cat remained behind, and it stared at Meike with such intensity they got to work right away.

Today was proving itself to be long and tedious, and they didn't have the company of a good book.

11

CAT HACKS

Meike found themself out on Sinnet street, in the way a thirsty traveler happens across a fresh spring. Their jobs from Griselda didn't take them out this far, which was a shame, as the salt air worked wonders for their sinuses. But no, she had them running closer to the heart of the city lately.

It was loud this time of day; the fishers were out in full force, hauling out nets of fish and other creatures—Meike spied the familiar curve of sharp claws in one net, and pink tentacles in another. And mussels!

They turned their gaze away from the fishing boats to Sinnet street itself, to the scattered shops and local vendors. The low fence surrounding the perimeter was the only thing stopping someone from walking out into the sea, a notable issue with a bar being so close to the docks. Other than fish and related tools, there were food vendors. Not much for Meike's diet, unfortunately, though soup was always an option. They had to be careful and only go for dishes containing seaweed and kelp, and only after asking what all went in it.

Meike ignored the alluring calls from the woman tending to a large pot, to a less than stellar shop. A tossed together sign that was equally tacked onto the building proclaimed itself to be "Krusty Joe's Crab Shack."

The interior of the building was more orderly than its exterior implied, which was a relief. The large net hanging from the ceiling and the mounted fish were a bit much, but the shelves were relatively tidy and easy to navigate. Meike happily poked around at the wares, and would've continued doing so in silence, had they not been spotted by the shopkeeper.

"Can I help you?" A long bearded and burly man behind the counter peered at Meike. He had eyebrows thick as caterpillars, and they "danced" on his expressive face.

"Yes." They placed a handful of silver coins before him, hand hovering over it before he could sweep the lot and send them out empty-handed. "I just need a good beginner rod, a tackle box, and ..."

"I'll do you one better," he said, giving them an exaggerated wink. "I've got a starter kit that goes for about, oh, for you I'll say five silver and thirty copper?"

"I don't know. I still need a rod."

"You get a free rod with your kit. A starter, mind, but it'll do what you need."

It all sounded too good to be true, and he mentioned nothing about bait. "You're the expert," they said, and the man beamed.

He disappeared behind the counter for a minute and came back with a sturdy tin box and a flimsy fishing rod. If Meike didn't know any better, they'd think he was moving inventory. But they weren't going to call him out, either. As customer and business, they both needed each other.

"I'll take it," they said with a sigh. The rod looked sturdy enough to last them through the next month or two. It was just something to help kill the time, and maybe drum up some extra coin for themself.

"Excellent," he said, sliding the coins away with his grimy fingernails. "Feel free to pick up one of our free guides." He winked, a more natural movement this time around. "And the best fishing spots, ranging from the guppy pond to the Dividing River. You'll want to start small."

That was fine by them, who preferred the catch and release way of fishing. They claimed a guide, a large folding map, and left the shop, pole resting on one shoulder.

Meike contemplated renting a boat for the day and setting up a distance away from the rowdy fishers, when one caught their eye. The so-blue-it-was-almost-black fur of a familiar cat. Patches had swapped its blue scarf for a bit of red, but they hadn't seen many other cat-people around here.

Still, they erred on the side of caution, slowly approaching the ragtag group—a collection of humans, reptilians, and their one feline friend. "Patches," they half-whispered, stopping beside a wiggling mass of tentacles.

The cat's ears twitched, and it glared at them with big green eyes, but softened upon recognition.

Meike held up their own rod, and the cat huffed. "I didn't know you fished!"

Patches glanced back at its companions, who were quietly laughing at the exchange, and sighed. It wiped its gloved paws on a handkerchief and sauntered over. Meike remembered the language barrier and shifted awkwardly in place.

It pawed at the air in what they recognized as sign language, but whatever magic allowed them to speak the "common" tongue did not extend beyond that. Patches hung its head to express disappointment and then snapped its fingers.

"I just wanted to say hi," they said, feeling sillier with each passing second. "Sorry to bother you, but I haven't seen you lately, and—"

Patches shook its head and resorted to finger spelling, but rather than thin air, a deep blue text clung to the air. *I've been at sea, it said. And that rod is going to fall apart the second you cast a line.*

"I bought it as a bundle..." They bounced it on their shoulder. Good enough for guppies, at least. "From Krusty Joe."

Patches let out a loud meow. *Honey, you got scammed. That's how he reels you in.* It slapped its knee and meowed at its own joke.

"Seems to happen a lot," they said, without the cat's obvious cheer. From courier to personal brewer, everyone promised one thing but failed to deliver. They still had hope for Maggie, but wanted to move on to something more practical. Actual potions and not glorified tea!

I'll get you a real rod. My old spare. Patches scratched its chin. *The box should be good. Overpriced, but it'll do.*

"That's great, but I'd rather learn your..." They swiped a finger in the air, but no color followed. "What do you call that?"

It's the mythic script. All mages learn it.

They did a double take. A mage that worked on a barnacle covered boat with salty sea lads? "Can you teach me how to use it? I haven't learned any cool magic tricks yet!"

Patches shook its head and wrote a simple, yet harsh, *No.* It jerked its head back to the rest of the crew. *Come by my place later.*

Patches kept a tidy home, perhaps due to it constantly being out at sea. Or maybe the cat just wasn't one to sit still for too long; the apartment couldn't have been larger than a tin can. Were they so inclined, Meike could touch the opposing walls with each hand.

They spun in a tight circle, taking in the rest of the room. A loft bed, a desk beneath, a low cabinet with a hot plate and kettle, dried fish and braids of garlic, and a shut door that either contained a toilet or storage area.

Patches took Meike's payment, a bucket of fish—a colorful array of guppies, all alive and swimming in water from the river, as requested—and motioned for them to sit on the only available chair. It was an old wooden thing with a cushion for comfort.

They watched in silence as Patches tipped the bucket over into a long trough beneath the tiny slit of a window. Fish or pets, it was hard to say, but not their problem either way. They nearly lost their rod when a trout latched on and refused to let go, even when Meike hauled it out to free it. Lovely specimen, but they didn't trust it with the guppies.

Satisfied with the arrangement, Patches leaned against the wall and flicked its fingers in the air. *I don't teach*, it said. And held up a paw when Meike protested. *But I can provide the tools for self study.*

"I'm down," they said.

Patches pointed at the box under its desk. Most of it was junk: loose string, old books, and soiled handkerchiefs. Meike went for the books, some of which they read as easily as any other, but the rest were in a foreign script. Patches' home country, perhaps?

It snatched a book from the box and tossed it up to the bed above, and pointed to one in the far bottom of the stack.

The book they retrieved was flimsy, and on the brink of falling apart. Random scribbles of the Mythic Script graced the front cover, but a quick foray into the book itself painted a clearer picture.

They frowned at the text and glanced at Patches for confirmation. The cat offered a sage nod.

The book was a glorified cursive guide, a skill Meike never thought they'd need, aside from signing signatures once a year at the most.

"You gotta be kitten me."

Patches let out a low yowl. Cat puns were out, then. *Children pick up the Mythic Script faster than adults. Provided they're magically inclined.*

"I've seen something like this before," they said, trying to sound scholarly as they leafed through the book.

There were a few differences from their childhood playbooks, such as the elaborate depictions of dragons, sea serpents, and wolfmen, rough parchment paper, and glorious footnotes! And a few food stains and tiny paw prints. Just how long ago was this broken in?

Patches huffed. *I expect to see your progress next time I'm on shore.*

Meike wiggled a finger in the air. They fingerspelled "Pickles" and concentrated, picturing the letters and distinct font in their head.

Nothing.

"I'm just warming up," they said. The cursive part was straight-forward; finding their magic was the real challenge. But ideally they'd speak to Patches in a matter more familiar to it. Not with magical text, but proper sign. It was something they always wanted to learn, both for their own sake and others.

Take what you want. I've been meaning to part with my childhood keepsakes.

Meike picked through the school books: a thin tome, more of a pamphlet, illustrating use of a fireball, one with a small child commanding a direwolf, a generic book on useful household spells, a stooped old wizard with a cauldron... They took all but the potion book and stowed the lot in their bag.

They may be starter spells for children, but they were finally going to learn some magic!

"Oh, and you promised me a rod. My other one..."

Patches held up a paw and disappeared into the closet. They leaned back to sneak a peek, but only saw darkness and the cat's furry back. The rod it carried was well polished and cared for, despite signs of wear and tear. Better than a new and pristine rod that couldn't withstand the weight of one fat fish.

Take good care of it. You won't find this level of craftsmanship at Joe's. With it came a handful of lures; fake worms and little feathered things.

"Thanks again, Patches! You're really nice." They reached out to pet it, but stopped short of touching the humanoid cat. Was that considered a microaggression? Pickles didn't like it either, but he was still a dog. But Patches...

The cat chuffed and petted them on the head. *Run along now, little one. And be careful out there.*

"I will!" They tripped over their own feet getting to the door, but straightened up without dropping their recently gained goods. Meike had to see Maggie in the morning for another exchange—mushrooms this time, thankfully, and more brewing. But they could sacrifice an hour or two of sleep, if it meant bettering themself and learning something concrete.

It was 2 AM by their watch, and the candle, formerly tall and glowing bright, was now little more than a stub. Meike yawned and got up to pace around the small room. It was roughly the size of Patches'

apartment, but a tin can that would surely burn like a furnace in the warmer months.

They hoped to be in a place of their own by winter, in a red bricked apartment on the nicer side of the city, with a hanging garden and a dank room for growing mushrooms, and little planters lining the window.

Meike gazed wistfully at their tiny slit of a window, where the moonlight offered a feeble beam onto their straw stuffed pillow. The bed called out to them like a siren song, singing of pleasant dreams and a much deserved break.

Instead, Meike lit a fresh candle and resumed writing practice. They'd tossed the writing guide aside after skimming through the key details. "Clear your mind, and channel your focus to your fingertips!" was the gist of it.

They were glad to be alone during the discovery phase, where they flicked their fingers a million different ways and even experimented with phrases for inspiration. In the end, meditation was the method that helped them the most.

Meike "scratched" the air with their nail, forming a ragged series of twists and into... They tilted their head at the word barely distinguishable as "potato". It was a lot like drawing with a computer mouse and not at all as easy as Patches made it seem.

But the important part was that it was possible. And if they could tackle the writing portion, they could conquer magic! Meike the Mage. It had a rather nice ring to it.

They rubbed their hands together and slowly pulled them apart. A glowing ball of light nestled neatly in their palms. It shimmered around the edges, threatening to go out with the slightest breath. The illumination spell was a traveler's best friend, and a low form of magic most people could learn with some instruction. Anniken would have good use for this.

Vibrating with excitement, Meike lightly bounced the orb into the air. It hovered for a few seconds and slowly fizzled out, taking its brilliance with it and plunging the room back into its cozy atmosphere.

It was the most useful of the simpler spells they'd learned so far, great for mushroom and rabbit hunting. What Meike really wanted to sink their teeth into were combat and support spells. And they couldn't shoot off fireballs indoors or on street corners (or so they assumed). The woods were out, for obvious reasons.

The taming book recommended birds, wild dogs, and rodents for beginners, with monstrous spiders, wolves, bears, and other creatures, for advanced students. Bunnies were the safer bet, but Meike dreamed of their very own armored bear.

And dream they did, as they gave in to exhaustion and retreated to bed.

12

ANYONE CAN CAST FIREBALL

Meike's catnap stretched into a full twelve hours; money wasn't the only thing they lacked an abundance of. The sun was out at full force by the time they hurried downstairs and almost ran smack into Anniken.

"If it's not you, it's the dog," she said, steadying them with one hand.

"Sorry," they wheezed, stumbling back and clutching their shoulder.

"What's got you in a hurry?" She looked them over, no doubt seeing the bags under Meike's eyes.

There was no time like the present! "I was up late, studying. I can show you, actually..." Meike cupped their hands together and envisioned a shining orb. The edges connected and a small sun materialized in their palms. And then it went sailing, aided by a light toss.

Anniken watched its trajectory. "Oh, that's a nice little trick. I learned how to make one of those in my adventuring group, but it's so fickle—"

"You already knew? Why didn't you tell me?" Meike's pride and joy sank down to shoulder level, where it reduced itself to a ball of fuzz. One, two beats, and darkness swallowed the light.

"Didn't see the point. You barely leave the house."

"I go out," they said. "Hunting, even. And not just for mushrooms!"

"Here, I'll show you how it's done." Anniken pointed a finger in the air, where a small bead of light formed and blew up like a balloon. Perfect form, brightness, and it cut an elegant path to the ceiling above, then down to her shoulder. It hovered there, like a tamed bird.

"What else can you do?" Was she familiar with the Mythic Script? Could she cast fireballs?

"That's the extent of it." She snapped her fingers, and the ball winked out of existence with a tiny pop! "Mages are fragile, and I'd rather be in the middle of the action. Monster taming is the one skill I can really see a use for." She cocked her head to the side, likely dreaming of her ideal partner. Probably something regal, like a wolf. "But I'd settle for just being able to converse with them. Works well enough on people."

"Coercion?"

"Well..." Her face took on a foxlike quality, full of unspoken mischief. "I suppose you could say that."

"Does someone in your adventuring group know of a..." What would they even call it?

"It's called 'Tongue of Nature.'" She rolled her eyes. "But yes. She's the group mage and healer."

"Can you introduce me to her?"

"Not without making it awkward. I joined this group a few days ago." She brushed an imaginary speck from her newly acquired and quality armor. Hard leather that provided ample protection for her chest, and a simple blouse beneath. The sword on her hip looked new, too. It had a sleek black handle, so they could only imagine the blade itself was just as fancy.

"And you learned all that already?"

"It's necessary if you're fighting sewer rats." She dropped a heavy bag on the ground and unraveled it.

Meike took a curious look and instantly regretted it. Thick tails the length of their arm laid inside, and the blood on the furry stumps looked fresh. "What are you doing with that?"

"It's for a quest. There's an ogre who treats them as a delicacy. Tastes like chicken, he says."

An ogre? Here in Laeford, or somewhere outside the city? They tapped their index fingers together. "I'd like to join an adventuring party, too."

"We're full, sorry. Party of five. A tank, mage, an archer, a sneaky cloak and dagger type, and then there's me! The lone blade."

"Why not...two mages?"

"A hedge mage at best," she muttered. "We'll be fighting goblins and many dangerous and otherworldly—to me, anyway, creatures. There's no room for pure supports, and you don't know the land well enough to be a guide."

The finger tapping intensified. "I can make potions."

"We could use a bunch of those, actually." She drew the bag of gore close. "Mana and health potions, and only the potent stuff. Or at least twenty of each, if you can't accomplish that. I'll pay you, but it has to be ready by the end of the week."

Meike, who'd been grinning as brightly as Anniken's light, felt a bead of sweat roll down the back of their neck. "I can get that for you. But how much..."

"Fifty silver, or two gold if you can craft greater healing and mana pots. Maybe throw in some poisons and salves to treat burns?" She jingled the coin purse firmly attached to her belt.

"That's um..." They chewed on their lower lip. "That's a tall order. I don't know if I can have it done that fast."

"Is that not enough? Steve said it was a fair deal, and he's an accountant. But I hear he likes to skim a bit from the top..."

"No, that's not the issue." They hadn't gotten that far in their lessons...yet. "I think I'd like your old sword. As part of the payment."

"What, that hunk of junk? I traded that in when I bought this." She patted the new sword. "I'll get you something better! And maybe a little leather to wear under your cloak." She slapped them on the shoulder and Meike groaned. "You're so fragile! Not even a glass cannon yet, just a frail little child."

"I think you're just really strong." If this were an MMO, Anniken would be fifty levels higher overnight, and have to babysit or power level them for two hours. If only this world worked that way...

"You'll get there. Anyway, I only came back to drop something off for the...Pickles." She held up a small, greasy bag. "Hearts and livers. Don't know how he can stomach the stuff, but—"

"I've heard enough, thanks." They could still hear him scarfing down the rabbit's. Ah, rabbits...taming would have to wait another day. "See you," they said, already practicing a series of scripts to run by Maggie later. Maybe they could bribe her with a whole roasted pig.

"Oh my," Maggie said, when Meike brought the order to her attention. "You've got yourself in quite the quandary, haven't you?"

"It's a lot, but I'm a fast learner. Check this out!" They produced a sturdier light, but couldn't mimic Anniken's grace. The ball merely bobbed above their head.

"See, you know magic! What do you even need me for?"

"Beginner level," they grumbled. "I still need to cast my first fireball!"

"Aw," she said, like a doting cat mom. "I'll show you later, but first we need to assemble our ingredients!" She held a tiny pair of glasses to her "face" and went through the list again. "I can pull these from my personal stores, but only if you promise to replenish them later. Most of it can be foraged, but the rest..."

Meike pointed at the Light. "That won't be a problem." They'd grown accustomed to the endless series of fetch quests and late night excursions. "Do you think it would be better to make the simpler potions or..."

"You don't hang around too many adventuring types, do you? Make fifteen of the simpler ones, and five of the greater. And twenty mana potions?" Maggie made an awful retching noise. "What sorry excuse of a mage can't manage their natural resources? No, make that four simple and two greater."

"But—"

"You said yourself that your friend was footing the bill. I'm using my expertise as a health professional to say that's an *absurd* amount of potions for one mage!"

They didn't have time to argue with her. "Who cares! I need the money."

"...right, I forgot you're *economically challenged*. I still think it's wasteful."

Maggie quieted down to help Meike get sorted. It was a big order, and they waited at the workbench as she left bundles of herbs—from dazzling shades of toxic purples, to crimson and periwinkle. Some dried, some fresh, some bulbous lumps that resembled turnips. And berries and flowers they happily identified as Bitter Nightshade, Foxglove, and Stinging Nettle.

"You'll be wanting these." She shoved a pair of thick rubber gloves into their hands. "For the sake of cross contamination, we'll save the poisons for last."

Meike rubbed their hands together. *This* was the kind of herbalism they craved! Actual potions and serums, not tea! "What should we start with first?"

"Healing. It's simple, and we can move on to the stronger batch while the first simmers. Here, I'll get you started."

She moved with alarming speed and ease, dissecting a green herb in a matter of seconds. Meike worried she'd lose a finger or two, but Maggie blitzed on until she had a large portion resting in her mortar. "They don't teach you *that* in school." She paused and tilted her head slightly to the left. Her version of a wink, they supposed.

From there it was on to the grinding process, and the lot deposited into a large cauldron she'd set up in a corner of the room. She set out a smaller one for Meike, along with lab equipment. Beakers and tubes, reserved for poison.

Maggie set her cauldron to a boil and stepped away after stirring it precisely five times. "We'll extract the weaker batch and come back later to double up." She sighed, wiping her hands on her apron. "I'll leave that to you. As for the mana..."

Watching her obliterate the red and blue herbs, Meike wondered if that was another form of magic or just something specific to her. Or maybe it came with experience. It would've been nice if she slowed down long enough to name and explain the herbs they'd be working with for the next few hours, but this was all part of her "flow".

"There," she said, setting down her knife. The tips of her fingers were now a rich purple. "I'll leave the rest to you. The brewing process is different…"

She dumped the grounded herbs, a mesmerizing mix of reds and blues, into the small cauldron. The major difference here were the two mana crystals she held out for observation. "Once the pot thickens, you crack these open and mix them in with the lot." She clinked the crystals together and whispered. "Pure mana extract. I'll show you how to make one of these later, though it'd be good to know a little alchemy in advance."

"Pure mana," they repeated.

"And the poisons…" She sighed and clutched her belly. "We'll save those for later. I'm all tuckered out, I'm afraid."

"I'll take care of the rest. I'm not sure about the berries, but I have an idea about the others."

"I'm going to have a snack and a little nap, and I'll come back to help you wrap up. There's still the cooling and bottling phase to worry about." And given the heft of the cauldrons, that might not be until the next day.

Meike picked up their knife and one of the green healing herbs. As they cut into it, all they could think about was the lack of electricity and all that came with it, and not just video games. A long task like this warranted pleasant background noise, either music or a podcast to keep them entertained for hours at a time while they chopped away.

If they couldn't find an alternative, Laeford or not, maybe they could find someone capable of making it happen. They eyed the mana crystals Maggie left behind. It was a shot in the dark, but she'd already shown that the crystals were enough to spark a flame.

…That was a form of magitech, wasn't it? There were a fair bit of more modern day appliances around the city, with the richer neighborhoods obviously having a monopoly.

The knife slipped, and Meike instinctively tucked the wounded finger into their mouth. They might have to leave Laeford to find out, but it would be worth it…

It was slow going with an injured finger, and the lack of windows made it impossible to judge the passage of time, but Meike hummed to themself to quiet their mind. They neatly arranged their piles of diced herbs into rows. Everything in perfect order, not a stray hair out of line. Symmetry at its finest.

Meike donned the gloves and pinched a berry between their fingers. These they could grind in the mortar and pestle, but then what? Just boil everything together? They glanced at the door, half-hoping Maggie would pop in and take over. But nothing; the door remained firmly shut.

Worse case scenario, she scolded them for wasting materials. But they would not give her a chance to do so. Fortunately, these were all fine to go straight into the mortar. Meike grinded the lot into a sticky paste and transported the mixture into a beaker. Add a little liquid, place on the burner, and…well, they were down one mana shard, but Maggie could always make more.

They were feeling pretty pleased with themself when she finally came down and saw the extent of their handiwork. Meike had painstakingly filled the provided vials with healing and mana potions, green and a light purple, respectively. Juggling a ladle and funnel was the hardest part of the process, but they got the job done with minimal spillage.

"Quite productive," she said, inspecting the pots. "Don't need me at all, don't you?"

Meike pointed at the beaker. In hindsight... "I covered it for now, but I don't know what to do about it."

"Same as the others. Just be careful you don't melt your fingers off."

"Is it acid?!"

She shrugged. "Would you like to find out?" She stood there, hands on her hips, until Meike moved to portion the yellow green fluid into vials. Despite being left to sit, it felt uncomfortably warm to the touch.

They nearly fainted when Maggie vigorously shook one of the vials. But the contents quickly settled down after the disturbance. Meike breathed a sigh of relief. The last thing they needed was permanent scarring.

"Pathetic," she said, tossing the vial onto the table. "There's no *spark*. But I'm not in the mood to teach you the joys of combustible poisons."

"Can I have a snack?" Their stomach was growling like mad.

"Oh, alright. Go rest up and I'll take care of the rest."

They spent the morning divvying up the mana and health potions into round, thin necked bottles. Meike liked the idea of tossing one mid-combat, like medicinal Molotov cocktails. Course, they'd need to substitute the glass containers for something more pliable and less deadly. If potions could be made into a gelatinous matter, perhaps.

Meike mused over this chain of thoughts as they weighed the bottles and carefully loaded the lot into their satchel.

"We should see about getting you a proper bag," Maggie said, voice dripping with disdain. She slid a chunk of foam into the bag, separating the small, fragile vials from the bottles.

"It's fine. I've done this a lot." Maybe not to this extent, but they'd grown careful over the past few weeks. Losing a week's pay because they smashed one vial and lost Griselda a customer was punishment enough.

"But you see why I insisted on a smaller batch?"

"Yes." They secured the bag and cradled it against their chest. The weight of it unnerved them, as did her silent reflection.

Maggie's disapproving gaze bore into their back as they hurried off, the bag clinking with each step. But the concern was unnecessary; Meike made it most of the way without incident, stumbling only at the sound of their name.

"Careful." Moira caught the bag slipping through their fingers. "Out on another delivery?" Her hair was freshly braided, the shells gone.

Meike was painfully aware of how much their own hair had grown out, and the lack of a proper comb meant it did as it pleased. They swallowed the lump in their throat and eased the bag out of her hand. "Yeah–mine."

"Your own?" It was small, but she was actually *smiling*.

"Oh, you know…" They raised one hand to tame the mass of curls sitting on their head, and had to switch back almost immediately to catch the bag. "I found a mentor. She's been showing me the ropes."

Moira edged closer. "Just the standard potions, or something spicier?"

"Yeah," they said, remembering the ginger tea. "I'm actually on my way to deliver these to my friend, Anniken. She's gearing up for an important dungeon run, and–"

"Sorry, but who did you say your mentor was?"

"Maggie…the flytrap."

"And is she taking care of you?"

"...of what?"

"Meike, your edges." She tapped her hairline. "Madame Claudette would never let me out looking like that."

"It's on my to-do list," they said. Right now, steady work and a full belly were more important. They could cry over their hairline later, and besides, Meike had no patience for braids and perms and the like.

"You better see to it soon, then. I'd like to invite you to work at my booth. Well, shared booth. It's a free for all for us lesser crafters, and I'd rather have the company of someone I can tolerate."

"I'd love to! Just give me a week or two to stock up." As soon as they paid off Maggie... "Gotta go, but I'll see you later!"

She considered them a crafter, her equal. Meike was so happy they could've jumped for joy! Minus the sensitive cargo, that is.

They spotted Anniken a few minutes later, loitering near a fruit stand. Meike raised their hand and opened their mouth, but the planned yell turned into a squeak at the sudden intrusion of a hooded figure.

The face beneath the hood was a bright crimson, its eyes conveniently shaded by the hood. Meike sidestepped the figure, but it followed and firmly planted itself in front of Anniken.

Was this one of those infamous daylight muggings they'd heard so much about?

Meike squared their shoulders and envisioned a stronger mage, like Maggie or Moira, faced with a similar dilemma. "I've mastered the art of magic, so watch yourself, buster." It sounded much cooler in their head.

"Lmao," it said, and jerked its head back. A long, pink tongue lashed out and clung to Meike's bag.

"Hey!" They dug their heels into the ground, but the amphibian effortlessly reeled them and the bag closer. It shoved Meike away and tucked the bag under its arm, belching and laughing.

"What are you doing down there?" Anniken, unperturbed by the blatant theft, extended a hand.

"That oversized frog stole your potions," Meike said, struggling to their feet. "Aren't you going to kick its butt?"

She glanced back at it and laughed. "Oh, that's just Casey. His whole thing is latching and knifing." She made a throat slitting gesture.

Casey raised a hand in acknowledgment.

"Could've said 'excuse me'."

He ignored them and rummaged through the bag. "Looks like everything's here, Zel."

"Who's Zel?"

"Zelamir. It's my alias," she said, ignoring Casey's ugly laughter. "Here's your payment." She handed them the coins first, saving the best for last. "You can skewer a few pigs with this."

The short sword was simple in design, but far sharper and sturdier than their knife. A stylized M was etched into the tang of the blade, and an owl's head was on the black handle. Meike bounced the sword in place and delivered an awkward slash through the air. It had a nice weight to it.

"Your form is all wrong," a gloomy voice from behind said. "You're going to slice your own arm off."

Meike jumped away from the tall boy with heavy bangs. "Are you one of Anni—Zel's friends?"

"Annie, huh?" The boy brushed his hair from his eyes. "You don't look like an Annie."

"Fuck off, *Harold*."

"The name's Sal Nightflayer," he said, to Meike. He could barely look at Anniken. The "cloak and dagger" rogue, if they had to guess. "Thanks again for sponsoring us, kind crafter. I'm always happy to support local businesses."

"Don't be weird, Sal."

"It's called *networking*, Zel." He grumbled to himself and slinked off, effortlessly blending with the crowd.

Meike glanced around for the rest of the party (like the elusive mage), but no one stood out. And Anniken and Casey were slowly edging away. With their bag...

"I'm going to need that back."

Anniken patted the bag. "Later. I have to distribute the goods."

"But—"

"Go break in your new sword or something."

"But that's my bag..." And they had some hope of meeting the entire gang, of rubbing elbows with a battle ready mage.

"Hey," the man running the fruit stand said. "Are you going to buy something or just stand there?"

Without a proper container, the most they could do were a few apples. The vendor looked disgusted, but still took their money.

13

DOG'S DAY OUT

Innkeepers always had the best room, second only to wealthy travelers and merchants. No drafts, rats, or surprise inspections. A fire always burned in the fireplace, and I got first dibs. Well, if only because the missus didn't take kindly to dogs curled up at her feet. Or on the furniture at all, if you wanted the truth of it.

The missus was an early riser, and the fire all but burnt out by the time I came to. She'd left two bowls out: fresh water and a meal of chicken, rice, carrots, the works. Your everyday peasant would think I ate like a king, but I only got the scraps paying customers didn't want. They dumped everything else into the alley for the strays to pick through.

After devouring yesterday's leftovers, I made my way downstairs to the kitchen. The head cook cussed me out, but she did that to everyone.

"Ugly little bastard," she said, coming at me with the broom. "Out! It ain't sanitary, animals in the kitchen!"

I held my ground and made a pathetic little whine, eyes going big as a pup's. That was the secret to melting Cook's heart. She gave her broom a half-hearted wave, but lowered it to toss me a chunk of sausage from her apron.

There was a little lint and hair on it, or, as I liked to call them, flavor enhancers. And it was delicious.

Belly full and ego stroked, I padded out the back door and had a lovely roll in some green stuff I found behind the inn. It was a beautiful morning, and the pigeons were out in full force. They crowded around the discarded food and slime, and after telling myself I wasn't going to do it, plowed right into the thick mass of bodies, sending them crying and cartwheeling through the air.

"Get a job, freeloaders!" One bird got its feathers all ruffled and flew in close, but I sent it stumbling back with a light kick.

My morning routine was very consistent and always kicked off by a stroll through the marketplace. Dogs weren't allowed unattended, but I had no owner. I was a free agent and did as I pleased.

I lingered beneath a cart, reminiscing on the day I made off with an entire duck. Those were the good ole days. And now I was skulking around, asking for handouts. My best dealer had to be Hal, the local butcher. He was a tall, wiry fellow, who gave rough pets and yelled when he talked, but he was a nice enough fellow.

"Who's a good boy, and why is it *you*?" He took my cheeks and stretched them into a farce of a smile. "Want some giblets and chops, huh, boy?"

An eager yip was the most I could manage, and it worked like a charm. He gave me some of the best cuts from a bucket he kept under his cart. Almost made up for the fact that a mean bastard of a horse tried to kick my brains in two minutes later. But sure, dogs were the villains here, and not the behemoths that are known to go buck wild and stamp on humans for sport.

"Piss off!"

The horse lowered its head and stared back, daring me to give it a reason to strain against its leash.

One of these days we were going to go at it, when he wasn't chained up like an ill-tempered dog (ha!). I settled for making a big puddle just a few hoofbeats away. He peeled his lips back from his chompers and whispered death threats in my direction.

I could feel his eyes on my back as I evaded the fuzz, snatching a small hen from a preoccupied vendor. It was like a game, except the penalty for losing was a quick death, or the fighting rings, if you were a remarkable specimen.

After crossing and backtracking a few streets, I took a breather in one of my favorite hangouts. The strays ruled this tiny alley and much of the abandoned street: all businesses that failed to thrive or were so overrun with rats and termites it wasn't worth salvaging.

The patron saint of lost kittens and pups, Sallie, laid on a makeshift altar, awaiting her offering. I dropped the hen into her pot, and we gave each other the sniff down. She smelled of cheap whiskey and fever dreams, so nothing new there.

"You good?"

She sighed and laid down. "It's hard out here, being the neighborhood emotional support dog." She had a far off look in her eyes, the sort that dreamed of a warm bed and meat set on low shelves. "It wears on you, seeing how badly your humans get run-down by the non-stop hustle. Chasing their dreams and burning out faster than a flame on a match."

"Damn, that's deep."

"I've been working on my poetry. One of the boys wants to start a zine. We're hoping to spread word of the dire straits afflicted on all of—"

"Yeah, lemme know when you're ready to distribute. One of my kids would be willing to help."

"Oh, that would be lovely, Pickles! We dogs can only go so far. A human—"

"Is the perfect mouthpiece, I know. Enjoy the chimken!"

"Yes," she said, tearing off a leg. "Freshly killed, too. Yes, I do believe you've earned a boost to vigor and strength. The cards are in your favor today, young one."

"Baller."

Yup, today was really looking up for yours truly! And they say dogs can't look up.

"Watch it, mutt," one of the long legs said, after almost stepping on me. I would've played the role of innocent pup, had the voice not sounded so familiar.

"What are you doing in my neck of the woods?"

Anniken sneered. "I was on my way to work when you barreled into me." She was always looking down on me, somehow immune to my roguish good looks and impish charm.

"Maybe you should watch where you're going, then." She swung her foot at me, but I easily deflected with a paw, almost breaking my 'perfectly normal dog, no funny business involved' facade.

I lowered myself back onto all fours and glanced around, but no one was paying attention to the tall woman abusing a small dog in the middle of the street. She certainly didn't look work ready; the leather satchel was missing, for starters, and her gear was a little too battle ready for sewing. But it was the sword at her hip that really tipped me off.

She patted the hilt of her fancy weed whacker. "I'm going to tackle the city's rat problem. You're more than welcome to join me, if you need a job."

"Tch. I'm cute. I don't need to work!" Not sure why it made her giggle, but I considered it a win. "Be careful. Those sewer rats fight dirty."

"Are you worried about me, dog?"

"No, it's just a friendly warning." I turned my head to show her I meant business. "You kids are too soft for your own good. Meike thinks bunnies are 'friends'. Vermin is what they are—oi!" She actually squatted down to pet me. My instinct was to bite, but I curled my lip at her instead.

"Who's the soft one now, huh?" Up close, I saw how well her sparring was paying off. Not completely shredded like yours truly, but she was growing baby muscles.

"Anyway," I said, nosing her away. "I have a hot date in a few hours and don't want to come in smelling like sewage."

"You *look* like you rolled around in one!"

"While you're here..." I sat back on my haunches. "I am in need of a tailor."

"Anything for you, darling Pickles," she said. I chose to ignore the heavy sarcasm.

"I want something nice. Like a red bow tie or bandanna."

"Why stop there? You'd look adorable in a little suit and tie." The delight in her eyes shook me to my core. Perhaps I'd come to regret this, but no one said being dapper was easy.

14

HEAD OVER HEELS

Anniken was busy, and Pickles was nowhere to be found. What that dog did while the rest of them were hard at work, they did not know. He generated little income (if any), yet always had a warm bed or meal waiting for him.

'I wish I was a dog...' Meike stabbed their sword into the ground. It dug in with surprising ease, and they saw that the soil had recently been upturned.

They pulled it free and surveyed the area. All around, in little clusters near trees or open spaces, were small mounds of dirt and discarded weeds. The holes were too big and disordered to belong to moles or other creatures, like rabbits. No, this could only be the work of a—

Obscured under a thicket of branches and vines came a low squeal.

Meike adjusted their grip, holding the short sword like it was meant for two hands and not one. Rabbits were too small to whack, and residual trauma from the man-eating plants remained. That left only boars, which provided ample fighting experience and monetary gains...they'd outsource the gutting and skinning, for obvious reasons.

"Little pig, little pig," they half sang.

Another squeal, and then a low grunt. The boar ceased all movement for a few seconds, before inching its snout from beneath the thicket. The nose twitched in several directions, followed by more grunts and the rare squeal.

'It's sizing me up.' It was in for quite the shock when it came running out, but Meike was prepared for it. They made a practice swing, felt the soft *whoosh* of the blade in their hands, and yelled "Fire!"

Calling out your spells wasn't a requirement, but the book suggested it for novices. The early attempts were like weak sparks from a lighter, though with a little emotion to amplify range...

A jagged ball of flame traveled down their hands and surged from the sword, traveling at high speed towards the boar. It chose that moment to wrestle free from the branches and let out a strangled squeal when it saw the approaching flames.

"Ahh..."

Smokey the Bear would not appreciate this at all, but at least the flames were contained. The boar, a young thing, almost a baby, really, thrashed around, emitting horrible screams that sounded all too human to Meike's ears. It rolled in the thicket, and when that didn't work, threw itself onto the grass. Round and round it went, but the flames only grew in number.

"I'm so sorry," they said, swinging the blade above their head. But also thrilled to have cast their first fireball, even if the results were quite terrifying for the poor baby below. *'Baby.'*

Their sword collided into the ground near the screaming boar. Just a little baby boy, innocent to the world around it. The most they could do was put it out of its misery.

But if it's a baby, wouldn't its mom be somewhere close by?

Meike came to this realization just as they sliced into the boar. It continued to kick for the next few seconds, but its breathing and screams died down to a pathetic whimper. And standing just a few feet away, puffs of rage streaming from its flared nostrils, was its mama.

They tried replicating the fireball, but all that came was sadness and the frenzied charge of a mother who just watched her beloved child go up in flames.

Running was out of the option, so Meike jumped and awkwardly clung to a low-hanging branch with one hand. They scrambled up the tree and perched on a sturdy branch, while the mama pig raged below.

She ran around the tree, squealing and headbutting it. But she couldn't climb, and for that, they were grateful. She certainly made an attempt, but gave up after the twentieth try.

"It's nothing personal," they yelled back.

She huffed and slowly retreated into the woods, probably to call reinforcements. Meike didn't stick around to find out; they got down and snagged the still smoldering body of the baby. It was only a little bigger than Pickles. The hide was ruined, but the meat was hopefully salvageable.

With no bag, they had to bind the thing with rope and carry it on their back. Meike took off in the opposite direction of the young boar's family, towards the river many dared not cross.

A family of deer turned and glared as Meike thundered past, adrenaline staving off exhaustion. They internally wept at all the delicious mushrooms they passed along the way—morels! Prized morels, in abundance and begging to be picked!

They teetered near the edge of the river, at the sudden eruption of rumbling beneath their feet. Either the deer ratted them out, or the boars had eyes in the trees—

Meike risked one glance back and stumbled to gain traction. Not thirty or fifty hogs, but twenty was overkill. Enough to run down all in its path. Hell, they stumbled over each other, and some even fell in the river, but hurried to rejoin the fray.

"It's just one," they called over their shoulder. It's not like they murdered her entire family, or anything—she could always have more!

They threw themself at the big hill, the last stop before absolute freedom and safety, and wish they had time to slow down and stow the sword away, but there was no time!

Not that it slowed down the boars. A few tumbled over during the attempt and couldn't get higher than the initial jump, but the mama boar ('*Sow?*') propelled herself forward on the false hope of beating Meike into submission and claiming her child's body.

She lunged and nipped at their heel, and they kicked her hard in the nose. The Sow let out one last squeal—a battle cry, if they ever heard one, and chomped down on Meike's ankle.

The pain was fleeting in the moment, but the desire to live was stronger. Meike cleaved one ear and a corner of the Sow's head off. She released them with a grunt, casting a scornful glare before free falling into the sea of pigs below.

"Oh Meike...what happened?"

When they collapsed in Laeford, it wasn't Maggie or Griselda, or even Anniken, who found them.

They tried to flex their foot and doubled over when pain shot up their leg.

"Careful," Moira said. "Don't strain yourself." She dabbed at their heel with a damp rag, taking special care around the bite wound.

"Is it bad?" They'd passed out more from exhaustion than pain, but their foot howled with unrelenting rage now.

Moira dropped the rag into a bowl of water. She'd taken them home, into a cozy studio apartment. A blue curtain hid the bedroom from view, leaving only the kitchen and living room. Light blues and browns were her aesthetic, paired with the charm of rustic furniture. And then there was Meike, stretched out on the couch, leg balanced in her lap.

"Not as bad as expected, but you'll want to stay off it for a while."

"Isn't there a potion I can take? And how long is a 'while'?"

"Potions are for adventurers and serious injuries, not little bites. This will heal on its own in three to five days." She bandaged the wound and gave their shin a reassuring pat. "We should find you a crutch. Can't have you putting pressure on this." She tapped the sole of their foot, and Meike fought back a squeal.

"I can hop…"

"Meike, please take care of yourself." She eased their leg onto the couch and rose to her feet. "Shin guards and some sturdy boots would have spared you from this."

They actually had a pair, but never saw the point of wearing them. The material was flimsy and provided no practical protection—no offense to Anniken.

"I didn't think I'd need them. I go in the forest all the time without a problem."

"Better safe than sorry." She offered her hand, just like when she found them.

Meike took it after a moment. When you were in a half-daze and ill, it didn't matter how help arrived, as long as it came. And they were glad to have her over anyone else at their rescue.

"Thanks again," they said, taking her hand—warm and soft. But the experience was over just as it was getting started. Meike rose easily on their good foot, but the pain came screeching back when they set the other down. It was easier to take if they related it to stubbing a toe. Quick to come, slow to fade. A dull throb...

"Easy now..." Moira looped an arm around their waist, steadying them, and Meike tentatively draped their arm across her shoulders. It was just like before, except they weren't total dead weight. "You poor thing. Are you going to make it home alright?"

They thought of the stairs to their tiny room and sighed. "I'll manage." But it wasn't *just* the stairs. How far was Moira's from the inn? And did they have to climb down to leave? It would be a long walk with or without her, and they were happier to curl up in a ditch somewhere.

"Meike?"

"Yes..." They tucked the injured foot behind them and hopped forward. "Where are we again? I think I blacked out on the way over."

"I live near the docks. There's a side road you take from the marketplace. It leads out to Sinnet, if you keep traveling east."

"East...Sinnet. Gotcha." They'd already forgotten about it. "And you got me all the way from the outskirts to here, alone?" They weren't exactly heavy, but she didn't seem half as strong as Anniken.

"I might've had a little help," Moira said. She was smiling at some inside joke Meike was unfortunately left out of. Perhaps it had to do with the bedroom curtain. Her lover, tucked in bed or engaging in quiet reflection while Moira played the role of doctor.

"Like a boyfriend?" It was the safest bet.

"Why, are you interested in applying?" One look at their face and she burst out in laughter. "I'm teasing! But no, I'm not seeing anyone."

They weren't sure what to do with that information either way, but it made them feel better. "But then, who?"

"My familiar," she said, like it was the most obvious thing ever. "You actually fainted when you saw her."

"...I did?" They were better off forgetting, if that were the case.

"My fault for not warning you. Most people don't react well to Effie."

"That's a cute name." Cute name for a scary demon.

"It's short for Euphemia."

She helped them down the mercifully short flight of stairs to the set of double doors. Meike heard the faint sound of ship horns behind it. The thin cracks in the doors told them it was daylight, so at least they wouldn't be hobbling home in the dark.

"I could summon her again, if you'd like. Would be much faster than me carrying you."

"I don't mind taking the long way home." They never had time to talk, truly talk. It was always a brief exchange during commutes.

Moira swung open the doors, inviting eye piercing light into the dimly lit entrance. "I do. I'm behind on work, thanks to our little excursion. But I don't like the idea of you walking back on your own, either..."

"Ah. I'm sorry."

"Don't be. Here, I'm going to summon her. Try to remain calm."

That was very hard to do when they couldn't remember why her familiar caused them to faint. Giant spider? Horned, gnarly demon with oozing sores? The possibilities were endlessly frightening.

Moira produced a small pewter figure, a goat, nestled in her palm. She mumbled an incantation and dashed the figure onto the street. Meike threw an arm over their face to dull the ensuing flash of light.

This they remembered. The blinding flash, the sudden heat, the smell of brimstone.

"How may I serve you, mistress?"

And that voice, soft, ethereal, *refined*. Oh, nothing like that could be a wiggling mass of flesh. No creeping madness, no rings of flaming teeth and eyes that covered every inch of their body.

So Meike lowered their arm, trusting the first incident was merely a result of nerves and debilitating pain.

"Euphemia, you remember Meike?"

"Am I to carry them?" The familiar offered very human-like hands–minus the soft white fur. Black fur covered her arms, chest, and goat-like legs. "Come now, little one."

Meike shrank back, forgetting their foot and almost stumbling back into the closed door. But Moira shoved them forward, into the waiting arms of the bipedal goat. Strong hands lifted them with ease, and Meike briefly came face to face with the goat and her bizarre eyes.

And then she hoisted Meike onto her shoulder, as though they were a small child. "There, there," she said, patting them on the back. And then to Moira, "Where do you want this?"

"Effie! Meike is a friend, not a sack of potatoes!" She came into focus. "Sorry about that. I've had her for a few years now, but she's still not where she needs to be."

"Please just take me home," they groaned. Being manhandled by a goat was one thing, but this was just humiliating. They'd be the laughingstock of the town, if they weren't already. "I'm staying at South Inn."

"Effie will get you there! That's like, six leaps from here."

"What do you mean by—"

Moira shrank to the size of an ant as Effie performed a mighty leap. That's how Meike imagined it must've seemed from afar, but it was terrifying on their end, on top of the sudden wave of nausea.

15

THAT DON'T IMPRESS ME MUCH

"Did you get everything? I told Effie to be gentle, but sometimes things get lost in translation..."

"I got it just fine."

With everything going on, they'd almost forgotten about the battered boar and their sword. She'd handed the boar over in a burlap sack, and almost skewed Meike with the blade.

Nothing out of the ordinary there.

Meike got the pig to Maggie before it spoiled, knocking off a chunk of their debt. She wanted more boars, naturally, but they talked her down by offering their paltry wages. At least until their foot was better...

"Alright, here's today's spread." If Moira noticed Meike's preoccupation, she made no mention of it. Or was too polite to do so. "Some of these I mixed for the occasion, others I couldn't sell for whatever reason."

She laid out her potions, mostly vials of lesser healing potions. The four round bottles she set out last were obviously a fresher batch. Greater mana potions.

Meike timidly arranged their collection of lesser potions. Moira had the advantage, being an experienced seller and all. Why would anyone want to buy cheap potions from a newcomer, and a foreigner, at that?

She gave them a little pat on the shoulder. "I was nervous my first time, too. It gets easier."

The booth they shared wasn't as heavily cluttered or close together as some others. No, all the "good" stalls were further down and selling potions and oddities—some even claiming to alter your body into spectacular creatures—or basic traits, such as height and eye color.

Meike yearned to browse and see what else they could aspire to, but they were confined to the shoddy stall that creaked and groaned in protest when they leaned against it. The stools that came with it weren't any better, but it beat standing. Fortunately for them, this corner of the market was shaded by a series of canopies, pockets of sunlight poking through.

It was actually kind of nice, all things considered. And the scary goat demon was nowhere in sight.

"What's a good selling rate for these?" They held up a healing potion.

"Five silver, twenty for the mana. It's what I charge for that quality. Anything more, feel free to double." She gave them another pat. "Just watch me, alright?"

The first customer of the day was a teenager in a cloak twice his size. He carried a longsword on his back and had tousled black hair.

"Good morrow, humble shopkeep," he said, ignoring Meike and focusing on Moira. He reminded them of Anniken's rogue friend. "I am in need of your finest healing potions and poisons, if you have any to spare."

"I mostly have these in lesser quality, if that's alright?"

"I'll take the lot," he said, and pulled out quite the heavy coin purse. Meike's eyes bulged at the sheer girth, the coins threatening to spill out when he opened it.

"Delightful!" Moira rubbed her hands together. "That'll be one gold and twenty silver. Do you need a bag?"

"No need." He whipped open his cloak, exposing a series of miniature holsters on both it and his belt, some already occupied. "But first..." He took out a single coin–copper–and held it out for Moira to inspect.

"Oh...you're one of those." The joy in her eyes died down as the boy lined the stall with rows and rows and copper and silver coins.

"I apologize for the inconvenience," he said. "This was my payment for my last foray into the mines." He paused his counting to glance at Meike. "Kobolds, you see. Foul creatures."

"Do you fight them alone?" She checked his math with more interest than the actual conversation.

"I'm a solo act," he said, holding his head high. "I work best alone."

"What other monsters do you fight," Meike interjected. "Slimes? Wolves? Giants?"

"All of 'em!" He lit up like a kid at Christmas, all smiles and childish glee. "I have a giant's toe necklace! Do you want to see it? The flesh was petrified–"

"Meike, shush. And after your payment, please." There was an edge to her tone that made both the boy and Meike avert their eyes.

"Yes ma'am," he mumbled, and doled out the remaining coins. His bag was much lighter for it. "Do you still want to see it," he mumbled to Meike, while he and Moira fumbled with their respective gains.

Meike leaned over the stall. "Big or little toe?"

He grinned back at them. "Big! It's the size of my *fist*. I call it a necklace, but I can use it as a flail in a pinch. It makes an amazing BONK when you bang it against a kobold's skull!"

"They've got hollow heads, then?"

He snorted. "Oh boy, do they!" He pulled out a horrific hunk of flesh from his belt. Dark pink with a flaky yellow nail running down one side.

"Ew," Moira said, cringing back.

"Cool!" Meike tapped the toe. It had the consistency of petrified wood, but felt heavy in their hand. "I wish I could buy one of these."

"Not for sale, sorry," he said, clutching his prized toe to his chest. "A giant's toe is incredibly lucky!"

"Not for the giant," Moira mumbled.

The boy regained his composure as he sauntered off, though there was a slight bounce in his step.

"You don't really like that kind of thing, do you," she said, once he was gone.

Meike traced a finger along a whorl in the wood. "I've never seen a giant or been in proper combat, so it's all neat to me."

"And you don't want to. It's not 'cool,' it's dangerous." She sighed and tied her bulging purse.

"Have you ever been in combat, Moira?"

"Only out of necessity. And I've faced greater things than trolls."

"...there's trolls, too?"

"Of course. They're smaller but far more aggressive. Giants tend to travel alone or in pairs, but trolls are..." She shuddered. "I lost a dear friend to a troll."

"I'm sorry..."

"Why? You aren't the one who killed him."

Things quieted down after that, the silence only broken by genuine customers and window shoppers. A handsome older woman, accompanied by a green heron, bought Meike's mana potions.

"I like your bird," they said.

Without a word, the woman stretched out her arm, and the bird hopped off her shoulder to settle on her bicep. It stretched its neck in greeting, and Meike marveled at the brilliant shades of green and red.

A green heron! They'd only caught glimpses of the larger and imposing species of heron, but it was even rarer to catch its smaller and vibrant cousins in the wild! And here one was, as someone's pet.

"Thank you!" They pocketed the polished silver coins. The woman didn't carry a sword or any type of blade they could see, but a bow—Meike stared unabashedly at her back and the unassuming dark cloak she wore. "So cool…"

"You have a real taste for adventure, don't you?" Moira's wares were almost wiped out.

"Not really…" Adventure was Anniken's thing. Meike valued stability and the mundane. It was safe, and foraging provided some excitement. "I wish I could go on a few quests. Nothing major, but I'd like to flex my magic skills."

"I see."

More customers trickled by, but few stopped to actually buy. Meike rearranged their meager potions as best they could, but the one customer who bothered to look them over bought up Moira's instead.

"Better luck next time," she said. They shifted away from the accompanying pat.

The way Meike saw it, they made out well with the mana potions alone. "Maybe I could try selling these in a bundle? Buy one mana, get two healing?"

"Up to you. I'd rather turn a profit."

"But wouldn't that make them want to buy more? I know I like freebies."

"You'd need a bigger supply to pull that off, otherwise you come off as desperate."

They kind of were, but she didn't need to know that. "I'll just make more potions, then!"

"That's the way, honestly. You could even scrape by with care packages. Those are big sellers, but you need variety, and I don't just mean poisons."

"Baby steps."

16

FERAL HOGS

SEASON 1 FINALE

The weekly orders were awfully light today, and most of it was pure parchment. Meike sorted through the pitiful collection of herb packets and vials. Together, it barely made a dent in their bag. "Is this all?"

"Haven't you heard?" Griselda tossed her newspaper down in disgust. "Wild boars have cut off our trade route."

"Wild boars? Why would they do that?" Meike had a very good idea, actually. A rather absurd one...

"Who knows? You can't even scavenge from the forest without one of the foul creatures assaulting you. The boys I usually send out have all come back bitten and bruised and scarred for life."

"Oh, no..." Meike's hands suddenly felt very sweaty. This couldn't all be about one little pig, right? They knew swine were smart, but did they really have the vengeful streak of a tiger?

"Yes, I had to dip in my personal supply to fix them up and fulfill a few orders. Fortunately, it seems someone is doing something about it."

"Like hunting parties?"

"More like slaughter parties. Why, just think of all the pig roasts and honeyed ham!"

Meike grimaced. There was no greater punishment than the smell of freshly turned chitins. They knew from personal experience—mom and the whole family, close and extended alike, loved pig intestines. Every major holiday, their mom bought a big bucket and combed through the mess, separating shit from flesh.

"It can't be that many, right?"

Griselda's eyes went big. "There's thirty, maybe even fifty, Meike! Big, strong boars! The markets will be heavy with meat!"

"Leaving now," they said, before she could go into further detail.

An herb shortage might not hurt someone like Maggie, and maybe even Moira; both had the cash flow to make up the difference. But for budding crafters like Meike and others like them...or anyone who heavily relied on trade or foraging would be affected.

'And it's all my fault!'

"That's one mean pig," Remy said, scratching himself beneath his robes. "I heard she's half-dead, running around with her brain matter exposed."

Meike collected his coin with a corner of their poncho, soon to be burned. "But does anyone know why?"

Remy spat a blob of phlegm onto the sidewalk. "Fuck if I know. But everything's going up right now. I'm gonna be eating rice and rats all week! Shit's ridiculous."

That was the general consensus this morning. The well off remained unaffected, but the ones at the bottom or just skirting by worried over the delays and potential price hikes.

"It's just pigs," Pickles said, slumped over a bench. "Can't believe people are working themself into a frenzy over it."

"It's a pretty big deal to some of us."

He rolled over, warming his belly in the sun. "If it were that bad, they'd send in knights and prepare the bonfires. People just want something to be mad about."

"Pickles, people have gotten hurt." One of the rumors floating around was how the boars swarmed and devoured a young adventurer. Sword and shield included.

"No one important."

Meike popped him on the bottom, and he shot a foot into the air. "If you don't think it's such a big deal, why don't you go help the killing parties?"

"I could," he snarled. "But what's in it for me?"

"...You're a very selfish dog, you know that?"

"And you're a chump. I don't work for scraps or head pats!"

"You don't work at all."

"Look, kid," he said, sitting on his haunches. "That reverse psychology crap isn't going to work on me. If you're so riled up over this, why don't you do something?"

"Maybe I will!" Wait. "Only because I want to, not because you...whatever." They had nothing to lose, and could even stand to gain a thing or two. Like money. And maybe a key to the city.

But first they had to figure out what was going on. Leaving Pickles to roast in the sun, Meike hustled to the market square. There was a small group around the request board, some familiar faces, some not. And no sign of Anniken in sight.

She'd at least had the decency to drop off their bag before plunging right into her quest, and would have to hack and slash her way through the boars to reach the city.

What a mess.

"Toe boy," they cried out, to the grim-faced youth swimming in his cloak.

He blushed and raised a slender arm in greeting. "My apologies. I never got your name."

"I'm Meike!"

"And I'm Theodore...though my friends call me Teddy." He popped his collar. Or at least tried to. "Are you to provide our merry band with donations?"

"Cease your prattling, boy." It was the woman with the magnificent bird. Her hood was down, allowing Meike a quick glance at her features. She had dark brown eyes and black hair worn in a ponytail. Without the hood, she looked younger than expected, somewhere in her thirties.

"I'm not giving donations," Meike said. "I want to fight with you."

Teddy and the bird lady exchanged glances. The bird broke out in laughter.

"Jasper, hush. Are you armed?"

"I have a sword and a few spells that may be of use."

"But do you know how to use it?"

Meike shrugged up to their ears. "Stick them with the pointy end?"

"Okay," Teddy said. "You can join us."

"Just like that?"

"We could use a capable meat shield," said the bird lady.

"Meat shield?"

"For the last time, Cassandra, you are not to use the new recruits as cannon fodder." This new voice belonged to a bipedal sheepdog. He crossed his arms and glared at her from behind thick bangs.

"Spoilsport," she mumbled. "I prefer to be called Cass," she said to Meike.

"And I'm Jack," he barked, drowning out the soft chit chat from the crowd. "If you've got a blade and killing intent, you're more than welcome to run with us!" He blew his bangs from his face, briefly revealing golden brown eyes. "Now, there's thirty—"

"I heard it's at least fifty," Meike whispered to Teddy.

"Try a hundred!"

"But that's all rumors from scared townies," Jack continued. "They may have the numbers, but we have the advantage, the keen intellect—"

"They ate a farmer and ransacked his wagon," a heavily tattooed man said. He carried a scythe taller than Meike. "It was all over in fifteen seconds. My aunt's friend's ex-husband's third uncle, twice removed, saw it all go down."

Jack massaged his forehead with a massive paw. "I swear to God, Deathbloom, don't embarrass me in front of the newbies."

"Sorry, boss..."

It was going to be a long day...and Jack said nothing about compensation.

Jack and the better armored adventurers led the charge through the city. Despite his eagerness to rush in with Cass and some of the deadlier looking crew, including a crocodile whose tail shimmied behind it, Teddy stuck by Meike and the timid Deathbloom near the back.

Judging by his kind, albeit clumsy smile, Meike was inclined to believe he was sincere. Or secretly wanted to claim them as a meat shield.

"Should the time call for it," he said between breaths, "I'll gladly lend you my toe."

Meike bit their tongue to stop themself from laughing. He looked so damn cute! "Thanks, Ted." A tiny giggle leaked into their tone, but Teddy took it well and flashed them a thumbs up. In that brief second, they saw him as the man he might grow to be someday—occasionally goofy but well-intentioned and willing to give his life for the misfortunate.

They hung back as the group filtered beyond the safety of the main gate and Meike froze. Since the day Pickles led them to Laeford, Meike hadn't ventured past this side of the city. Hadn't seen a need to, til now.

"Everyone, together," Jack yelled. "At the end of the day, it's just a bunch of pigs—*ow*." He swung a fist at the boar tugging on his leg. "Mages and archers, in the middle! Everyone else, up front!" He kicked the boar into the air.

Chaos followed and Meike briefly found themself alone as Teddy jumped into the fray, hacking and slashing into a pair of boars. The beasts formed a ragged semicircle along the outer perimeter.

"'Scuse me," Deathbloom said, intercepting a boar in mid-jump. His scythe neatly cleaved into the poor animal, sending a spray of blood that its fellows wore as a badge of honor.

Meike conjured up a ball of flame and bounced it from hand to hand, searching for juuust the right moment...there! They tossed it over Teddy's head, into a cluster of boars. They took no joy in the killing, but the sound of their once defiant nature devolving into squeals of terror was...oddly exhilarating. Was this what Pickles felt in the heat of battle?

Charred and mad as hornets, the singed boars surged towards Teddy, the one thing standing between vengeance. The boy growled and swung his sword in a wide arc, clipping one boar and critically wounding the others.

A quick glance at the battlefield gave them a good count of the score. Jack, Cass, Teddy, and most of the front liners were holding their ground. A few were injured, though nowhere near as bad as the prone bodies scattered among their feet. Hard to believe butchers were greedily sharpening their knives to carve up this bunch. And that was assuming the bodies were collected in time...

"You alright," Teddy screamed into their ear. He wiped a smear of blood (not his own) from his cheek.

"I just remembered something!" The whole reason they were even out here. "Zombie pig."

"Zombie...pig?" The blank look in Teddy's eyes faded when a boar snuck a bite of his shin.

"The half-dead sow." What if this was all a cleverly crafted ruse, and she was leading a separate attack from the back? The exit Meike used for foraging wasn't as heavily secured. What few guards patrolled Laeford settled petty disputes or watched the roads. Lexanard was at peace, and the surrounding kingdoms were on good terms with each other.

"I don't know what—ow, stop that!" He kicked the dead boar off his sword. "What's this about a sow?"

Meike fumbled with their own blade, saving the integrity of Teddy's cloak from a voracious pig. It shrieked indignantly at the gash in its side. "...Nothing."

"Make way! Make way," Jack shouted, ignoring the boars and waving at the makeshift battalion.

"Fuckers," Cass growled, but fell back.

"What's happening," Meike said. Not even ten minutes had gone by, and they'd only gotten a little taste of the action. There were still plenty of boars, too.

Jasper swayed on her shoulder, and Meike saw a dash of blood on the bird's beak and plumage. "The calvary is here," she snarled, and said nothing further.

Meike didn't have to wait long; mounted knights lined the road in threes. They mowed down the boars with ease, beneath blade and hooves. A hoard of boars decimated within seconds.

"All that good meat," Teddy wailed. "What a waste…"

"Forget the meat," Jack said. "What about the *glory*?"

Meike elbowed their way to the front and stretched to the tips of their toes to get a better look at the procession. Impressive armor, all shiny and polished like they were fresh from the blacksmith.

And then they saw the head, bobbing up and down with glazed over eyes and lolling tongue. And the missing portion of its ear and skull. But the height was all wrong, unless the sow grew over twelve feet.

"That's her," they said, jostling Teddy's shoulder. "*The sow.*"

"Holy cow! Where's the rest of her?"

That question answered itself two minutes later, when the proud knight pranced before them, the sow's head held high on a pike.

"Oh, come on!" By all rights, the final blow should've been theirs! This was to be their showdown, a clashing of hooves and steel!

"Meike? What are you doing out of your hole?"

Anniken sat astride a magnificent white stallion, angled so that her legs hung from one side. She had an arm around the knight accompanying her, a knight who wore not the standard silver, but heavy black armor. A wicked helmet fashioned in a dragon's screaming face obscured all but their eyes—a vivid cerulean, beautiful despite the harsh, stony gaze.

The knight placed a dangerously clawed glove on Anniken's hip, a gentle gesture that did not escape Meike's discerning eyes, and leaned their head near her ear.

And Anniken giggled, soft and giddy, and murmured back an indescribable phrase. A girl a little younger than Teddy ran over to help Anniken down, mindful of her left leg.

"Ann—I mean, Zelamir…" Meike rushed towards her, wary of the knights, more so the one dismounting behind her. The squire they ignored entirely. "Are you alright?"

"Why wouldn't she be," Teddy exclaimed. "Do you know who that *is*?"

Meike glanced up at the knight, who waved back. "No?" They would remember such a knight. The knight was at least 6'2," possibly taller; everyone looked tall when you were 5'4".

Teddy let out a high-pitched whine that made all the dog people shudder. "Women want her! Men want to *be* her! The magnificent—"

The knight coughed, and with a dramatic flair, removed the helmet. They wore their jet black hair in a single braid, a lovely contrast with Anniken's white blonde locks. "Annie, would you care to introduce me to your friend, or should I?"

Anniken cleared her throat. "This is Laken. Laken the Great, Laken the Magnificent…"

Laken waved at her to continue. "Please, I love when you talk me up."

Teddy bounced in place while Anniken stumbled. His face was red from the exertion of not finishing for her. "Dr-dr…"

Anniken sighed and rolled her eyes. "Laken, slayer of wolves and dragons." She glanced at the beaming knight behind her and blushed. "She also happens to be my girlfriend."

17

LOVE ON A WIRE

SEASON 2 PREMIERE

"Anniken's dating a knight..."

Two hours had passed since then, but the news was still very fresh in Meike's mind. No one else batted an eye; Laken was an out and proud lesbian, and could whip the ass of any man who dared to challenge her.

As told by Teddy.

"For now," he said. "Laken has...quite the reputation with the ladies, if you know what I mean." He nudged Meike in the side, almost dislodging the boar they were struggling with.

Somehow, the responsibility of clearing the bodies all fell on Jack's crew, while the knights were free to gather in the city. And that included the ruined corpses...the icing on the cake was a squire demanding they mop up the blood and gore.

"I don't." They had an idea, but Anniken was their friend(?); speculating on her private moments felt...invasive.

Meike looked to the salamander, Casey for help. He was the only one of Anniken's party who bothered to stick around or even reveal himself.

"Laken runs through women the way a baby goes through diapers. Everyone knows, and everyone thinks they can tame her!"

"Oh...that's sad."

"It's romantic! I can clear a dungeon, but I can't talk to a girl, and it's driving me up the wall! I want to pick up women! In or out of a dungeon, I'm not too picky."

"Kid's a simp," Casey said, eying Teddy with something close to contempt.

He placed a hand over his heart and glared back. "If respecting one of the greatest knights of our times makes me a 'simp,' then so be it!"

"That boy ain't right," Casey said, and snapped up a fly when it drifted close.

"Can you *not* talk about my sex life while I'm here?" Anniken tossed a boar into the slaughter wagon, nearly nailing Teddy in the head.

"Sorry, miss," he said, growing pale. "I didn't mean anything by it."

"Our relationship isn't your business, either." And yet, there was a flicker of doubt in her eyes.

"Is this pipsqueak bothering you, babe?" Laken loomed over Anniken's shoulder. She was a giant compared to Teddy.

"*P-pipsqueak?*" Teddy stood on his tiptoes. "I am neither a pip nor a squeak!"

"He's a simp," Casey said, turning to Anniken.

"And proud of it, I'll have you know!"

Laken wrapped an arm around Anniken's shoulders. "There's only a few left." She pointed her chin at the mountain of meat. "Meike, you're more than welcome to join us."

"What about me? I want to hear about your latest exploits!"

Casey grabbed Teddy by the back of his cloak and hauled him back.

"That boy is almost as bad as Pickles," Anniken said, peering down at them from the white stallion. Laken and Meike walked on either side of her.

"What happened to your foot?"

"Nothing serious," she said. "I sprained it earlier, doing something silly."

"But you never do anything silly."

"I don't want to talk about it," Anniken yelled over Laken's soft laughter. "Ask me about my girlfriend."

Meike glanced over at said girlfriend, who was staring straight ahead. She wore the smallest of smiles. "How did you two meet?"

"Well, that's less embarrassing." She sighed and fiddled with a lock of the horse's mane. "I saw a poster of her jousting and thought 'I want to be just like her someday.'"

"...What?"

"I don't believe in idolizing popular figures, but if I have to be like anyone in this world..." She glanced at Laken. "Then why not her? But soon I wondered if I didn't want to be *with* her instead."

"But how did you actually *meet*?"

"Meike shush, I'm pining."

Could she maybe pine faster? Meike almost regretted asking, but they were awfully curious. "Is this why you want to be a knight?"

Laken smirked. "I told her to at least consider it, but Annie said no."

"Knights have a lot of responsibility."

She winked. "They don't get to quest as much, either."

"I like the freedom to come and go as I please, and I've developed a taste for adventure." She reached for Laken's hand. "Knights don't travel often, do they?"

"No, unfortunately. Though we do when we're needed, like now..." She scoffed at the blood bath behind them. "Imagine my surprise when I saw Annie facing off with the Sow Queen herself!"

"We were handling it," Meike said.

"It's too big a job to leave to casuals." Laken lowered her voice. "And between you and me, the Commander wanted to save face. A ragtag bunch of guards and adventurers fighting off a boar infestation? Say what you want, but us being here bolsters the confidence of our citizens."

Compensation seemed less likely now.

"Laken," Anniken said, once they were safely within the city.

"Yes, my love?"

She stretched out her arms. "I want you to carry me."

Meike peeked at her ankle. "It's not very strong, but I have a potion—"

"No, it's quite alright." Laken lifted a giggling Anniken with ease and held her princess style.

It seemed impractical to Meike, mostly with that armor. "How long have you been dating? Does Pickles know?" Not long, they hoped. It would've come up in conversation...somehow.

"Pickles?"

"He's my dog. Meike's been puppysitting for me."

"*Puppysitting*?" Had she mentioned them at all, and how?

"Anyway," she breezed on by, ignoring Meike's pained expression, "it's been...two weeks, I think?"

"Sounds about right," Laken said. "But I'm terrible with numbers, and the days blur together for me."

"Time is an illusion, yes." She kissed Laken's impressive jawline.

Meike closed their mouth, astonished. "It's only been two weeks?" Them moving in together would be peak lesbian culture.

"More like eleven days, but I rounded up."

Maybe Teddy was right. But they both looked so happy together. And Meike was being pushed back by the sudden influx of Laken's sea of adoring fans. They ducked down a side street, leaving the merry couple, crowd, and pounds of pork behind.

Unsurprisingly, Pickles was right where they left him, stretched out on his back, paws tucked close to his body. Meike considered poking his belly, but they wanted to keep all their fingers.

"Pickles?"

One eye shot open, and he rolled onto his side. "How did the pig run go?"

"It went great! We..." Well. "They're all dead!" They left out the bit about fresh meat and the upcoming feast. He could cry over the scraps later.

"Cool." His eyes drifted shut. "Did you bring any for me, or do you get a kick out of depriving hardworking dogs of sleep?"

Meike leaned on the bench. "I want to go on bigger adventures. I...didn't do much in the fight."

He snorted, and one ear flopped open. "Shocker. You need better gear and spells."

"I can cast fireball! And tame monsters. I think..." They wanted to. The opportunity just hadn't presented itself to them. Yet. "It'll be easier on me if I can tame a boar to fight for me."

"Start small."

"But boars are as small as it gets!" Like that poor baby they mangled and later fed to Maggie. Just how small could they possibly go?

"Think smaller." He perched on the edge of the bench, hind legs swaying gently in the air. "Like bunnies."

"Here we are, back at the scene of the crime," Meike muttered into their fist, picturing a mic.

"What's that?"

"Just thinking out loud."

They stood at the top of the hill, one tumble away from the tree line and creeping triffids. Somewhere beyond all this was another group of boars, either unaffiliated with the deceased group, or the remnants of. And Meike wasn't too excited to rush out and greet them.

But the potential for greatness was just within their grasp...

"Look kid, I know how tempting it is to jump into the thick of things. And a boar would be a great starter pet—you'll get very far, and can even double up by using it as a mount." He pawed at his cheek. "If you were Anniken."

"She has all the luck, doesn't she?" For someone who was adamant about leaving, she sure was thriving. Made for them, indeed.

"It's determination that drives her."

"I'm plenty determined! I've pushed myself beyond my comfort zone."

Pickles stared at them with half-lidded eyes. "If you were a pup, I'd eat you first."

"Hey!"

"Sorry kid, thems the breaks." He yawned and stretched out, turning into a giant furry loaf. "Go tame your bun. I've got your back."

It was a bit late in the day to go hunting for bunnies, but Meike was familiar with the habits of rabbits. And could spot a burrow just as easily. But it seemed wrong, shocking them out of slumber, especially for mothers and their kittens.

What they sought were the scrapes of bucks, hardy opponents but with less at stake. A doe will fight tooth and nail against intruders to protect her nest, even against fearsome snakes and birds.

As luck would have it, they didn't have to search too hard or far for the perfect "mark". But they *did* come close to infuriating a boar, a larger and scarier rendition of the Sow.

It was covered head to hoof in crisscrossing scars, snorting and pawing at the base of a tree. Tucked out of view and line of sight was the cowering figure of a lesser animal, all hope and sense gone. This was the end of the line for it, and it was only a matter of time before the boar broke through and snatched it up.

But that's where Meike's expertise and generosity came in!

They didn't need Pickles' help for this task; the boar was so focused on its task that it didn't notice Meike sneaking up behind it, and so was a sitting duck when their sword slashed into its flank. It whipped around with an indignant squeal, but was met not with Meike's blade, but the heft of Pickles' axe.

"Get wrecked," the corgi said, having cleaved clear through the boar's skull. Still, it made one last effort to bodily lift Pickles into the air, but he held firm and kicked it in the eyes.

Meike let the two have it out and threw their poncho over the rabbit, which was just coming to. It squirmed and kicked, and didn't relent when they eased the fabric off and cooed at it.

"Don't worry, little one. I don't want to hurt you. I just want to be friends."

They hadn't touched the animal taming book since that first night of study, but the basics were laughable for an adult. And it was only a bunny...

"I need you to wrap this up in a doggie bag," Pickles said, blood dribbling from his lips. The boar was...not in a good way; the strike from Meike greatly injured it, and Pickles' handiwork took it completely out of commission.

No one would ever believe a corgi was capable of taking down a 200 pound boar. No one outside of this world, anyway.

"I wouldn't. There's going to be a huge pig roast tonight."

"...And you didn't think to run that by me?" He almost looked mad enough to swing that axe at *them*.

"They still have to clean and prep everything. And I didn't want to be around while they did."

"Oh, come on! I could've supervised! I love this stuff!" He stamped around on his tiny paws, shaking the axe in the air.

Meike fought back a giggle for fear of stoking the flames. He was so cute! "I'll help you drag it back into town if you help me with the rabbit?" They held out the squirming bundle, but Pickles huffed and withdrew.

"Don't underestimate me," he said, and lifted the boar with surprising strength and speed. He half-dragged, half-carried it by one massive hoof slung over his shoulder. "*You* carry the rabbit."

That was perfectly fine by them.

They cradled the bundle in their arms and carefully unfurled one end to expose the rabbit's rapidly twitching nose. Meike gradually revealed more and more of its face until they saw its darting eyes. The squirming had long stopped by now, but they weren't willing to release it or relax their grip. The rabbit was bound to flee the moment it thought it was safe to do so.

"I'm going to take it home with me," they said to Pickles, taking a breather from hauling his kill, back pressed against a building.

"You do that." He wiped his brow with the back of a paw. "I need to find a butcher."

"Enjoy the feast."

"Are you really not going?"

They shook their head and clutched the bun closer. "I need to finish taming it. I think it might be injured..." The rabbit held one leg close to its belly.

"But you're gonna miss out on all the food!"

"I know, but I don't eat pork."

Meike only wanted a nice tossed salad. And one didn't need to go to a pig roast to find that.

18

PRINCE WITH A THOUSAND ENEMIES

"You're safe here," Meike whispered to the bundled rabbit. They set it on the bed and carefully unfurled it.

It laid still, curled in a loose ball. Its sides rose and fell in rapid succession, much like its nose. It wasn't hard to see why; it was more than just its hind leg. Blood stained the bad leg, flank, and belly.

"He really did a number on you, huh?"

The rabbit jerked, eyes opening into thin slits. It didn't look ready for a fight, not that it would get very far.

"Let's get you cleaned up."

Meike left it alone and quickly hurried out to collect a bowl of warm water and a rag. The rabbit was right where they left it when they returned, eyes closed and paws pressed into its cheeks.

It flinched when they touched it, but relaxed as Meike cleaned the blood from its fur, seeking the source of its wounds. There were two big ones that they could see on the leg and side. Fortunately, neither reached the internal organs. That leg concerned them more than anything; a broken bone was harder to mend, and Meike didn't know if potions were an efficient method of treatment for animals and monsters.

Logic told them no; that's how it worked in most video games, unless the monster was under your control. It was considered a party member at that point. But as Anniken loved to tell them, this wasn't a game.

She'd also failed to convince them entirely.

Meike patched up the rabbit as best they could, applying a poultice to its wounds to help staunch the bleeding and prevent infections. It behaved rather well, though much of its complacency could be attributed to fear of the large predator looming over it.

It curled up in the poncho while Meike left once more—this time to procure food.

"Hold up," the cook said, when Meike stopped by the kitchens. "You can't be down here."

"I just wanted to take something to my room."

She squinted at them. "You're the grass eater, aren't you?"

"Vegetarian! But yes. Do you have a head of cabbage and a few carrots?"

"Cabbage and carrots." She shook her head. "By all rights, I should send you off. You're going to starve yourself."

"I'd like a pastry, if you have any of those."

"Pastry, they say!" She huffed and briefly disappeared in the back, coming back with a wilted cabbage and an assortment of veggies that were close to being tossed out. "I'm happy to supply you with rabbit food, but pastries and things—those are for *paying* customers."

Meike kept their mouth shut on that; them being here meant they *were* a customer, albeit not one that normally requested food directly from the kitchen.

She'd done them a kindness and provided Meike not only cabbage, but carrots, a radish, and a stalk of celery. They transformed the salvaged veggies—carrots, radish, celery, and the cabbage—into a large, dry salad. Dressing was something they had to make on their own, but this was probably the one time where that wasn't necessary.

Their little rabbit friend might not take too kindly to oil and vinegar.

They fed it bits of carrot and a cup of the cabbage. It took only a cautious nibble at first, but was soon chomping down and tearing the food straight from their hands. If its leg wasn't so beat up, it would've taken the entire bowl and retreated under the low bed.

"I suppose I should name you," they said. Not something as grand as Hazel; that was too much to place on a single rabbit's shoulders. "How about...Fern? Or Sage! Or, no..." Meike snapped their fingers. The perfect name... "*Saffron.*"

The rabbit wrinkled his little nose at the name, but calmly ate the rest of his meal, and soon was drifting off to sleep.

"Aren't you precious," Moira said, squatting to pet Meike's new friend.

It would be a while before Saffron's wounds fully healed. He limped and favored one leg, but he was up for following them out to survey the festivities. He kept close to their heels, cowering every time strangers ventured close.

A bit too shy for a battle buddy, but rabbits weren't their first choice for that kind of work, either.

"His name's Saffron. I found him while foraging and took him home with me." He leaned his weight into their shin. Was that his subtle way of calling them out?

"Aw, what happened to your leg, little guy?"

The perplexed bun glanced at Moira and tilted his head back to peer at Meike, who shrugged. "He was getting bullied by a boar."

"A boar!" She rose to her full height, dusting the ends of her robes. "Not the horde outside the city, I hope."

"Oh, no. This one was alone. But I was involved in the skirmish earlier..."

Downtown was exactly what they expected, although not quite as red. Signs boasting a big feast lined the streets and doors (promoters worked quite fast), and the stench of burnt flesh and fur riddled the air.

Meike chose a safe distance away from the main area, where all the people were like tiny ants, flitting from booth to booth and carrying hunks of meat. Some even had entire heads of corn, which was almost tempting.

"Are you going to join them?" They spotted two tall figures, one tall and adorned in heavy armor.

"No, I think I'll sit this one out," Moira said, folding her hands at the waist. "Not that I don't like pork, but things are going to get...chaotic soon, and I'd rather not be a part of it."

"Oh. Food fights?"

"I wish." She wrinkled her nose. "Drunks."

"Oh. I don't drink, either." They scooped up Saffron and held him close to their chest. He didn't seem to mind being handled, though only stayed still in short bursts.

"Were you really out there? Weren't you scared?"

A tiny figure ran after Laken, either Teddy or her young squire. It was hard to tell from this distance.

"Not really. I had the support of other adventurers."

She smiled and held out a hand. "Well, I'm glad you were safe."

"Maybe you could join us next time."

"...There's going to be a next time?" She stared at her hand and lowered it. "I don't know, Meike..."

"You should! You and...you and Effie." The thought of the goat demon filled them with dread, but they could tolerate it as long as the two had a common enemy.

"Effie's not built for combat," she snapped. "It's a thing most mages do, but I don't see my familiar as a tool for battle or grunt work. Euphemia is my friend and companion."

"I'm sorry..." Saffron kicked his good leg and quieted down once they set him free. "My friends—" *Were* they friends? Or just acquaintances? "—are moving on without me. I just want to keep up."

"I thought you wanted to learn magic and heal people?"

"I want to do both. I want to be strong and have people rely on me." Strong like Pickles, quick-witted like Anniken.

"You do you," she said, kinder than before. "I'll support you from afar."

"Aw, what a cutie..." Anniken stooped down to greet the bunny, cautiously extending a hand for him to sniff. She notably favored her "good" hand, having learned one lesson from Pickles.

"I can get you a rabbit," Laken said, staring at it with mild interest.

The party ended sometime last night, long after Meike curled up in bed. They made a tiny bed for Saffron out of a box and some hay, and either from sheer exhaustion or his mending wounds, he slept through most of the night, stirring once or twice to paw at the door.

Couldn't quite take the wild out of the rabbit so easily, it seemed.

Laken and Anniken dressed casually, yet seeing her stripped of armor did not make the knight any less imposing. Unlike Anniken's homemade garb, Laken's gold and blue tunic was of higher quality and design, as close to "high fashion" as one could find around here.

Cotton fabric that looked soft to the touch, like silk. And clearly tailored to suit her height and build, in the most flattering way possible.

Meike shuffled awkwardly, painfully aware of their dingy poncho and cheap attire. They tried to keep themself clean and presentable, but next to Laken they felt like a peasant.

"No, that's fine. He's *adorable*, but you know I can't take a pet with me on the road."

"He's not a pet," Meike blurted out, before they could stop themself. "Saffron is a battle buddy."

"Is that so?" Laken smiled and shook her head. "A battle bunny..."

"Laken." Anniken stood up and lightly nudged her in the side. "Be nice."

"What? You'd trust a bunny in battle?"

"You don't know what Saffron is capable of," Meike said.

At the mention of his name, Saffron leaned back and stared at them, mouth agape, as if to say "Don't bring *me* into your spat, human."

"He has a broken leg and looks to be the runt of the litter."

Meike stooped down to cover the rabbit's poor ears and spare his dignity. "He can't help how his body is! And rabbits make for great boxers. He may not be able to square off with a boar, but he can take on a weasel or two, can't you, Saffron?"

Saffron looked visibly disturbed by this point, but wasn't actively fighting against the cause, either.

"I want a dog," Anniken said. "Or something comparable."

"Darling, you have a dog. And he's cute as a button!"

"Pickles isn't—okay, maybe a little. But I want something sweet and loyal. He's too independent."

Meike failed to see how that was a bad thing. Furthermore, how could one be too independent?

"We'll find something better, I'm sure. You'd look simply marvelous on the back of a crystal reindeer!"

"A mount and a pet, all in one."

"Battle buddy," Meike insisted, though Anniken and Laken were caught up in their own little world.

"I'd love to get one for you, or at the very least, guide you, but..."

"You have your obligations, I know." Anniken stepped behind Laken and turned her around, for what Meike assumed was a stealthily placed kiss or other act of intimacy.

They weren't on a high traffic street, but Laken stood out like a torch in darkness.

"For you, I would drop them all," she said, and Anniken sighed. "Cut my hair, give up everything I own, move to a faraway country...if you came with me, of course."

Her promises also sounded suspiciously like a certain Colombian singer...that had to be a coincidence, but like with Casey, something wasn't quite right.

"Should I leave?"

"Yes," the two women snapped in unison.

Meike scooped up Saffron and hurried down the street before steam and cheesy affirmations of love enveloped it. They were happy to run into Teddy, who hastily stuffed a spying glass in his cloak.

"Ah, my good potions crafter! Fancy meeting you here!"

"Give it a rest, kid," the sour-faced Cassandra said.

Meike wasn't too thrilled to see her, but they were glad for the distraction.

"What are you two doing here?"

Teddy scuffed his boot on the ground. "Me and some of the other adventurers wanted to recoup our losses." He puffed out his chest, and Meike knew a speech would soon follow.

But Cass kindly interfered.

"The boy and I are more solo acts, but we figured it would be faster and more...efficient to work together. Perhaps pull together a full party."

"I'm looking for a party too! I can be your support."

"And that?" Cass waved a hand at the bunny cradled in their arms.

"He's a battle bun—battle buddy."

"Could also be a decent meal, in a pinch."

"He's not for eating! Just give him a chance to prove himself."

"You say that now, but can you keep up once we're beyond the meadows?"

Meike turned to Teddy. "What else is there?" The man-eating plants, boars, and wolves they knew about.

"Treants, dragons, dire wolves, giant spiders, goblins, kobolds, thorn tailed weasels, bears, centaurs..."

"Generic fantasy monsters? That's not so bad."

"Gener—please don't say that in their vicinity! You'll provoke them."

Cass snorted. "Worried, little Teddy?"

"No, and I'm not little! I'm growing."

"I can also tame wild monsters and animals. I'm a valuable asset."

"Just focus on healing for now," Cass said. "And leave the rest to us. Though we still need a tank..."

Teddy cleared his throat. "Meike's friends with Laken. They can ask her."

"I am *not*." They were barely friends with Anniken, but Laken was for sure a hard no. "And anyway, I don't want to bother her."

"It's okay to be afraid," Cass said. "I may present myself as an impenetrable woman, but I respect and fear a knight of their standing." Teddy nodded in agreement.

"I'm not—okay, maybe a little, but that's not why."

"Then I'll ask her!" Teddy ran past them, but Meike grabbed the end of his cloak and tugged, gagging and holding him in place. Just a little something they learned from Anniken.

"I know someone who can help."

Granted, he was more of a bruiser.

19

GOTTA WALK BEFORE YOU CAN RUN

"**S**ure, I'll do it."

Pickles hopped off the raised cushion he shared with a golden lab and Afghan hound. The lab whined after him, but the Afghan held herself with more dignity. More specifically, she turned her nose up at Meike and lightly huffed.

Tough crowd.

At least Pickles looked happy to see them. His tail was wagging, and he wore a big, goofy grin on his face.

"Great! We still need time to prepare, two days or a week at the latest."

Teddy wanted to go on an "epic adventure," though Cass insisted they keep it small. Meike fell somewhere in the middle, but as the team medic, they wanted to be stocked before fully committing to a longer campaign.

It might require some help from Maggie or Moira.

Oh, Moira...it was a shame she was so skittish about adventuring, when that goat of hers was perfectly outfitted for excursions. They could clear a lot of ground with Effie alone, and it would be one less mount to consider.

"Just call my name and I'll be there." Pickles winked, and Meike wasn't entirely sure he was sincere or not. One could never tell with him, but maybe the company of his lady friends put him in a better mood.

It was the same with Anniken, actually...

She was off doing her own thing, presumably with Laken. Meike hadn't seen either since that day, but expected the Knight to return to her duties soon.

Saffron pawed at Meike's leg, and they stooped to collect him. He bounced back remarkably fast, but still wasn't at his best yet. Outside of battle, the rabbit would prove a worthy ally for foraging edible foodstuff and sensing potential danger. Not entirely tame, but he'd given up on escaping, at least.

"Your first adventure! Aren't you excited?" They said that more to themself, abating fear of the unknown and placing faith in their companions. Teddy and Pickles seemed unlikely to leave them for dead, though Cass remained a mystery.

And they were all trained fighters...

"I'm excited," they said, petting the bunny's head. "Do you want to go outside for a bit?"

Saffron's ears pricked up at that, and he squirmed to be let down. That was as good a response as any, but his spirits dampened when they attached a makeshift leash around his midsection. Might be a good idea to pester Anniken to fashion a proper harness for him.

Like a cat, Saffron flopped onto his side and refused to budge for a good two minutes. Even then, he only hopped a few times before settling down and repeating the arduous process.

"It's gonna be like that, huh?"

He thumped his leg in displeasure and turned to heavy weight in Meike's arms. He remained broody until they stepped out of the city proper, surrounded by a sea of grass and endless trees.

The grass glistened with dew and residuals of a recent rain, and Meike was pleased to see the precious Mica Caps and other mushrooms of interest. They tied the other end of the leash onto their wrist and stopped at the nearest cluster.

Saffron happily sniffed and dug at random spots on the ground, occasionally snapping up a dandelion and other tasty morsels.

Meike's basket grew heavy with not only Mica, but Chanterelle and the much coveted oyster mushroom—two great clusters that would last them a day. They piled on wild berries, a few wild apples, and assorted herbs for cooking and potion brewing.

It wasn't a lot, in the grand scheme of things, but everything in this basket would last Meike a good week or two, more if they picked up supplementary ingredients at the market or during their travels. Saffron could live off grass in a pinch, but they wanted to keep him as well fed as possible.

"Only roots," the kindly farmer asked, when Meike stopped by her stall. "We've got pickled cucumbers, eggs, pigs' feet, and boar jerky. You'll want to be stocked up on your proteins!"

Meike felt themself turning green at the very idea. "No, thank you. I don't think jars are safe to carry on the road."

"Why not? You're taking a cart, aren't you?"

"I think we're walking, actually." That would be better on their feet than the initial trek to Laeford. Meike was fairly confident they could handle that same trip now; city life kept them on their toes.

She supplied Meike with two heads of cabbage, carrots, and tubers. Their basket was getting heavy enough to shift from arm to arm. Such was what they were doing when a familiar face flagged them down.

Meike smiled when they saw Moira, but frowned at her goat companion. They would never get used to that. To her.

"Why, hello there," she said, leaning over her stall. "It's funny seeing you on the other side of the counter."

"Oh, you know me." They held up the overburdened basket. "I'm actually here to stock up for my trip! I just need a few potions. The rest I can brew myself."

"A very smart move." She winked. "Is it more for yourself or your companions?"

"I'm shopping for them. I shouldn't need to use much for myself, but it's good to be prepared."

"Make extra." She slipped a tiny vial into their hand, small enough to pinch between thumb and forefinger, the contents a bright teal. "I hope it doesn't come to it, but if you ever find yourself at the edge of your rope..."

"I'm fine, really." They pushed it back, but Moira held her hands aloft. "What is it?"

"Why, it's alchemy. What else?"

"Alchemy..."

Moira urged them closer, and they obliged, scrunching their shoulders when her lips brushed their ear. "It's a literal lifesaver."

Their eyes widened. True magic! What else was possible?

"I keep one on me on the rare occasion I need to leave the city."

"Oh Moira, I can't take this! What if you need it?"

She pulled a duplicate from her cleavage, attached to a glistening silver chain. "That's why I keep backups, like any respectable alchemist."

They stored the mini potion in their pocket, nodding resolutely. "I'll guard it with my life!"

"...please be careful. I'd hate for anything to happen to you."

Meike bowed, almost sagging from the weight of the basket. "I promise!"

"What's up, cats and kittens?"

Pickles presented himself in a tiny cape, a fitted leather jerkin, and a matching pair of greaves. His axe was polished and slung over his back, and one of his lady friends gifted him the tiny bandana around his neck.

Meike would've killed to have their phone. Not that they had many followers, but it was easy to make a cute dog go viral.

Cass was less impressed, her lip curled and finger pointed in Pickles' direction. "Meike, what in tarnation is this?"

"That's Pickles."

She sighed, closed her eyes, and massaged her temples. "Our 'tank' is a dog. Our 'tank' is a dog named Pickles."

"Pickles Barkenshire Jr.," said the owner of the name. "My mother wandered onto a ship and stowed away in a barrel of cucumbers—"

"I didn't ask for your origin story!"

"I do," Teddy said, squatting and extending a hand. "Enlighten me of your travels, brave pup."

Pickles spat into Teddy's open palm. "Get the fuck away from me."

"Hey! You said you'd be nice."

"This is me being nice," he said, as Teddy hastily wiped his hand clean on his cloak. "The only thing that tops white women's tears are cute dogs."

"I take great offense to that, Sir Barkenshire."

"Anyway," he said, swiveling back to Cass. "I know I'm cute and my belly looks soft as hell, but I am a force to be reckoned with."

"Don't defer to her! I'm the leader." Teddy swept his arm through the air, but didn't stamp his foot. He wasn't that far gone yet.

"I'm not putting my life in the paws of a dog."

Pickles reared up on his hind legs and took up his axe. There was a flash, a glint of metal, and the solid *thwack* of the axe embedding itself into a wooden sign.

"I've got a bite force to match."

"Alright," Cass said, having examined the axe and forced it out of the wood. "You've got good form and range. Your bite pressure remains to be seen, but I'm willing to work with you."

"Hold on, I didn't agree to this. As your leader—"

"All in favor of Pickles joining our merry brand of murder hobos, say 'aye'!"

Two human hands and a paw shot into the air. "Aye!"

"You can't just overrule me!" He did it—he stamped his foot and swung his arms in the air. "I have some valid concerns and objections!"

Cass snorted. "The solo player wants to play leader all of a sudden?"

"I'm the handsome, charming one! I am the glue that binds us together!"

"So, where are we starting first? The mountains, Slime Canyon, or the mines," Cass said.

The other two were self explanatory, but the mountains held an air of mystery.

"What's in the mountains," Meike said.

"Giants and wolves, mostly," Teddy said, edging his way back into the conversation. "You'll occasionally find the odd troll, but they like to stick closer to the mines. Unlike the kobolds, they actually put in the work."

Meike didn't like the idea of being crammed into a small space with a bunch of trolls, even with Pickles and the others around.

"I'd like to try for the mountains."

"It's not easy," Pickles said. "Might be better if we clear Clark Meadows first."

"Mountains," Meike insisted. They were intimately familiar with the meadows, saw the same animals and monsters every time. "And shouldn't we check the quest board first?"

"Laeford isn't the only place where requests are put up. You'll find them out near outposts. But it doesn't hurt to look…"

Meike and Teddy ran off to the quest board, leaving Cass and Pickles to talk shop.

The board was covered in dozens of requests, some old and faded, others piping hot. But most were local or only went as far as the meadows.

"No mountains?"

"It's a ways off," Teddy said, lifting a newer request to peek at the one below. "Sometimes you'll get lucky and find a quest chain that eventually leads you out of the city, but those get snatched up fast by guys like me."

"Do you think it's worth going without a quest?"

"Yeah? It's like a treasure hunt. *And* you get to test out your skills!" He placed his hands on his hips. "We could pick up a few quests here and carve our way through the meadows, like originally planned, go to the next city over and collect more quests, then double back to turn in this first batch."

"That sounds like a lot, Ted." They wanted to dip a toe, not go swimming. "We don't have nearly enough supplies for something that big."

"It'll be all right, I assure you! We forage if we have to and restock in the nearest town or inn."

Easy to say when it came to food, but not so much with potions and other supplies.

"I can try," they said.

"Excellent!" Teddy took a request, glanced at it, and rolled it up. "We'll start in the meadows and work our way to the mountains."

Meike wasn't too thrilled about that, but Teddy was in charge here, and Pickles and Cass were in agreement.

"It's efficient," he said, unrolling the paper. "We cut our way through the meadows, taking down ten giant wasps, five boars, and two thorn-back bears."

"Did you say a *bear*?"

"Yeah. Big black bears, covered in purple vines."

"That's a small list," Pickles said. "I can take out half of those mobs on my own."

"Is everyone ready, then?"

Everyone raised their respective appendages and followed Teddy, beyond the city gates.

20

SPIRAL OF ANTS

"Ten giant wasps, five boars, two thorn-back bears," Meike repeated to themself, as the merry band of adventurers trekked into Clark Meadow.

Pickles led the way, followed by Cass, then Meike and Saffron, and Teddy and the Rent A Mule at the rear. Cass' green heron, Jasper, flew overhead, occasionally disappearing beyond the tree-line. He was their scout, the main alert to trouble ahead.

"Watch out, there's a cluster of those plants inching by." The procession paused as Pickles drew his axe.

Meike froze in place while everyone got into position. What turned into a somewhat relaxed stroll was now looking to be a small scale battle. Everyone carried a blade, even Cass, who was normally a bow and arrow user.

What followed next was mostly a blur. Pickles took on two of the shambling plants at a time, while Teddy casually hacked one to pieces. Cass moved with greater grace than the other two, dealing swift, effective blows that expended less energy. She assisted when needed, but was the first to sheath her sword.

"Since that rabbit of yours isn't fit for combat, it can help collect loot."

Saffron disappeared behind Meike's legs.

"We can do it together," they said, and the rabbit timidly revealed the tip of his nose, before bounding after his owner.

The plants dropped an assortment of herbs, gruesome body parts, and even partially digested meals. Meike collected even that latter half, just under the possibility it contained useful alchemical ingredients.

"They always drop trash," Teddy said, as Meike filled the sack on the mule's small cart. "Sometimes you'll get lucky and find a coin or two, but it's mostly stuff for the compost heap or crafters."

"What do you normally do with it?"

"Sell or leave it, naturally."

How unbelievably wasteful! Just how much lost potential did Teddy leave strewn about the ground?

Pickles and Cass were more sensible, discarding outright trash, like random shoes, tattered bits of clothing, and a rusted can. Still, Meike monitored their teammates during the next batch of monsters, perhaps the most lucrative:

Boars.

The one time they felt comfortable partaking in the fight, Teddy and Pickles utterly obliterated four of the boars. Meike had the pleasure of striking the fifth, but Teddy rushed in and finished it off with one thrust.

"Hey, I had that one!"

"Gotta be fast," he said, smirking to himself as he wiped his blade clean.

"Don't be greedy," Cass said. Unlike the others, she hung back to snipe from afar and assist in loot collection.

It was the usual with boars: heaps of raw meat, their hides, and other odds and ends one might want to keep. Cass loaded the five bodies onto the cart, with the implication that they would be gutted, skinned, and cleaned.

Meike scribbled a message on a tree, using the Mythic Script:

5 boars down, 10 wasps and 2 bears to go!

But things turned sour at the wasps.

At the heart of the meadows, deeper than Meike ever dared to venture, was a thick cluster of trees that stretched as far as the eye could see. They'd have better luck observing from the city proper, atop one of the tallest buildings.

The trees were thick, close to the giant Sequoia trees they'd only seen pictures and videos of online.

Hanging a few feet above their heads was a poorly concealed wasp nest, bigger than the simple constructs made by mundane wasps. Meike backed away from the trees, observing a hovering insect near the nest. It certainly seemed to observe *them* in turn.

When they heard "giant wasps," it never occurred to them that these would be bugs the size of domestic corgis. The wicked stinger the wasp flexed was comparable to Meike's hunting knife, both in length and width. One well placed sting from that, and you were done.

Saffron whimpered and retreated a safe corner under the cart, where the Rent A Mule steadily munched on a patch of grass. Meike edged away as well, but drew their sword. Not that it mattered; ignoring its freakishly large size, the wasp bobbed and weaved with ease in the air, and would prove a formidable opponent.

Cass notched an arrow and leveled it at the wasp. Pickles and Teddy waited like children eager to hit a dangling pinata.

"Meike," she said, voice calm like the prepped bow. "I need you to fire at the nest when this arrow flies."

"But—"

"Just do it," she snapped.

Meike fumbled with their sword and raised a trembling hand towards the sky. This was going to turn nasty fast, but they had two options: trust their crew to take down the monsters, or turn tail and run.

"Now!"

The wasp dove towards Cass, stinger extended. But the arrow struck first, sending it back with a series of shrieks into the tree trunk, where it was left frantically kicking its legs and beating its wings.

Meike launched a fireball at the nest, successfully setting it ablaze and popping it free from its perch. Three wasps came crawling out, angrily buzzing and searching for the source of chaos.

The closest person just happened to be Teddy, who sliced the nest clean in half when it tumbled into his vicinity. That was all fine and well for a bit of sport, but his blade was too long to effectively stop the assault in its tracks.

The first wasp shrugged off the flat side of Teddy's blade and dove for his face. The second wasp circled around him, and the third performed a tidy barrel roll and shot between his legs, tangling itself in his cloak.

"Begone, you damn bees," he cried, flailing his sword in the air.

Pickles tackled the wasp in Teddy's cloak, sending the boy sprawling and at the mercy of the two attacking his face and torso.

"I wouldn't have stood there," Cass said, from the corner of her mouth. "Calm down, Ted! I can't get a clear shot!"

Teddy uttered a low shriek, dropping his sword as the wasps overcame him. But he didn't go down alone.

An arrow caught one wasp in the midsection, spurting inky black blood into the air and over Teddy's prone figure. Pickles snagged the other seconds after it impaled the boy. He shook the wasp with vicious glee, throwing the bug onto the ground before pouncing and ripping it to pieces, scattering limbs and shells onto the ground.

"Let's get him away from here," Cass called, coming to assist. "Meike, have your potions at the ready! We'll need to remove the stinger."

Together, Cass and Meike carried him away from the battered remains of the wasps, and laid him on a bed of grass and wildflowers. His cloak spread out like disheveled bat wings, and his sword was safely within reach. They elevated his head with a burlap sack and tended to his wounds.

Meike couldn't stomach the sight of blood and gore, but Cass offered to work the stinger free and staunch the blood. She even wiped his wounds clean, and Meike handled the rest, applying a poultice.

"Do you know how to sew, Meike," she said, watching them hard at work.

"A little. My grandma tried to teach me when I was younger, but I wasn't interested." They would consider doing so now, if they were going to play the role of doctor.

"I suggest you take it up." Cass flexed her hands, cleansed from Teddy's blood. "Even I know how to sew. It saves me the trouble of relying on others. Or talking to them..." She shivered.

"How's the kid doing," Pickles said, sauntering over. He wiped a little blood and spittle from his mouth. He was lucky to only have been grazed; his armor caught the worst of the stinger. He declined treatment, in favor of licking his wounds.

The broken stinger laid at Teddy's side. A full two inches pierced clean through his chest, missing his heart and other vital organs.

"His breathing is normal. He's just sleeping it off."

Pickles kicked Teddy's comatose foot. "Sleeping on the job."

"How long will he be out for? I don't want to make camp here."

"Maybe an hour? It's really up to him." Meike wasn't in favor of waking him up, but would happily do so if more wasps arrived. Perhaps then they could slip him a healing potion. "We still need seven more wasps," they said, mopping sweat from his brow. "Can we do it with just the three of us?"

"I don't see why not. Pickles can guard Teddy while we snipe the rest."

"Wait. Just the two of us?"

"Technically three. I'll be providing backup if they get in range."

"I don't know..." Meike respected wasps and bees, which was why they avoided the insects whenever possible. Teddy's demise only reinforced that.

"We'll fight fire with fire," Cass said, collecting her fallen arrows. "I'll even join you."

"Do you know magic too?"

Cass waved a hand at the arrow she held, and flame danced along the shaft to tip. "I'm more of a hybrid than a true mage, but my aim always strikes true."

"Elemental weapons! Can you teach me that?"

"No. Now come along." She trained her bow at another nest, several feet above the previous. "And don't worry about keeping score. The auto-counter does that for us."

"...Auto-counter?" Meike glanced around, but saw only unbroken wildlife.

"Focus on the opening, if possible. It doesn't have to be perfect."

How would Anniken or the honorable Laken handle giant flying pests? Nothing short of finesse, they assumed.

They launched a fireball at Cass' instruction, neatly singeing one side of the nest. Cass fired an arrow into the first of the escaping wasps, and a second into the one behind it.

Working in tandem, Meike and Cass whittled down the number of fleeing wasps down by five. Arrow, fire, arrow, fire.

"Only two more to go!"

This was substantially less scary, and Meike was even putting their magic skills to good use! Patches would be proud.

"Good job, kid." Pickles patted their knee, which was the closest he could come to petting their head. "You too, Cass."

"Don't feed me that shit, old man," she spat. "I'm no amateur, unlike that boy."

Teddy groaned in his sleep. "I said no Bavarian cream...only glazed..."

"Come on, help me take down the rest. I want to move the boy somewhere safer and set up for the night. We can clean up a few of those boars."

Meike's stomach turned at the idea. They cut the stingers free from the growing pile of wasps and claimed two intact carapaces. Surely there was a use for these...

"Do you see a nest?"

Try as they might, Meike couldn't make out one through the mass of branches and leaves. Perhaps those first two acted as sentinels? There had to be more high up. But short of climbing, they had no idea of how to reach them.

"Forget the nest. We'll just have to scout for stragglers."

Meike peered at the narrow passage between the trees, too tight to allow for anything other than single file.

"Do we have to?"

"Do you want to finish the quest or not," Cass said through tight lips.

"Yes, but—"

"No nuts, buts, or coconuts," she said, and took the plunge into the dark tree-line.

Meike sighed before following her. Barely noon and already it felt like the world's longest day.

"Cass, wait!"

"What?" She trained her bow at something beyond Meike's vision. Tiny glints of sunlight poked through the canopy of leaves.

"You mentioned something about an auto-counter?"

"Alchemy. I'll explain later. Give me light, will you?"

Meike illuminated the area and choked on their own breath.

Eyes. Dozens of beady little eyes glared at them from the trees and low bushes. Big eyes, little eyes, glowing eyes, *hungry eyes*. Some came in twos and eights, others belonged to creatures far too big to be a wasp.

Cass stood firm, though there was tension in her voice when she spoke. "Don't panic. One last tussle and then we run, all right?"

Two wasps. They only had two wasps to go.

Flame enveloped Meike's hand as they followed Cass' bow. The surrounding eyes subtly retreated deeper into the encroaching darkness. Or were the monsters waiting for the best moment to pounce?

Meike didn't allow themself to dwell on the matter, and focused more on blasting the barely obscured wasp.

It all happened so fast, and though Meike floundered, Cass acted with precision and speed, taking out the final wasp before it reached her.

The monsters watching from the darkness winked out one by one, an excellent time to make an exit.

"Ten wasps," Meike said, half-curled in the cart.

"I hate them," Cass said, dropping the remains mere inches from Meike's head. Another carapace and two semi intact stingers.

"You aren't hurt, are you?" Pickles pressed his wet nose against Meike's hand. "You screamed like a pair of wild banshees."

"Alive and well. How's Teddy?" Cass loomed over both of them, frowning and wiping her hands on a handkerchief.

"Sleeping beauty is safe and sound. A little too sound, if you ask me..."

"Of course he is. Not that I expected much to change in the course of twenty minutes." Cass sighed and rolled up her sleeves. "Butchering time!"

Meike shot up so fast their head spun. "No!"

"What do you mean no? If we're going to wait for Teddy to rouse, we may as well make good use of our time."

"Can't we wait a day or two? I don't think the meat is going to go bad that fast!"

"Ideally, we'd have to bleed it at least overnight. I figured there's no harm in getting a head start."

"It's stinky and gross, and I don't want to watch you gut a dead animal!" Not the mention the smell could attract more monsters.

Cass sighed and rolled her eyes. "Then don't look. Or get in my way."

"Pickles!"

One ear perked up. "Sup?"

"Help me!"

"I don't see anything wrong with it, unless the boy recovers before night. Five boars is a lot to get through in one day."

"Fine," she said, putting away a wicked looking knife. "I insist we keep the bear carcasses intact. Those will sell well if carved by a professional butcher."

"I don't care, just don't do it near me," they said, settling back in the cart.

"Good, we're in agreement. The bears are mine!"

Pickles hopped in place. "Now hold on…"

"Gotta be quicker than that, dog!"

Meike left the pair to bicker, and looked upon poor Teddy, twitching in his sleep. Saffron hopped onto his lap and scurried away when shooed. The rabbit, so far, was not living up to his status as "battle buddy".

Teddy tossed his head from side to side, contesting his demons. "No salsa," he groaned. "Just white, pinto, half and half steak and chicken…no I don't want veggies or cheese…sour, pile it on!"

…Was he dreaming about food again? Meike hovered a hand over Teddy's face, just as he started to tantrum over the lack of fresh chips. And brought it down upon his cheek.

"This place sucks," he wailed, sitting up and simultaneously drawing glances from Cass and Pickles. "I asked for sour and they globbed on all this gross guac—" He pressed a hand to his face and gazed up at Meike in astonishment. "Did you slap me?"

"I thought you were fooling around."

"Sleeping on the job!" Pickles waddled over and seized Teddy by the trousers, half dragging the boy from his makeshift pallet.

"Easy dog," Teddy groaned as he struggled to his feet. "Don't I at least get a snack first? I almost died, after all." He looked so small and vulnerable without his cloak and tunic, and had very little in muscle definition, aside from his arms.

Cass tossed him a chunk of dried meat, which Teddy crammed into his mouth and chewed on as he hastily dressed. There was a curved line where the wasp stung him, an angry red smear on otherwise pale flesh.

"You took out the wasps in my stead," he said, nodding in Meike's direction.

"Yes, and it was very scary. Please don't collapse near the bears."

"Your concern is appreciated, Meike," he said, adjusting his pants. "But I am a man and can fend for myself." The red mark of the waking slap stood out on his cheek.

"Okay," they said, and fell in line with the procession.

By all logic, Cass should be high on their list of priorities; she proved herself to be more than capable, but she was a ranged fighter, unlike Teddy and Pickles. She wore even less armor than Teddy, all cloth and not a greave in sight. Meike was better protected, and that was only thanks to Anniken's insistence.

But after today, they were definitely going to order sturdier gear and spells, if possible.

They loved their poncho and intended to hold onto it, but leather armor would get them far. It might even resist wasp stingers and bear claws.

"What are the bears like? And what do they drop?"

Teddy yawned and stretched his arms above his head. "Bigger than your average bear, mean, covered in purple thorns that glow as if bathed in moonlight. They've got huge teeth and wicked claws!"

Meike's eyes glazed over as he went on. "And how many pairs do they come in?" Earth logic said bears were more solitary creatures, unless it was mating season.

"Alone," Cass said. "It's rare to see them in groups, unless...you know. And it's not that time of the year. Makes our job harder."

They breathed a low sigh of relief. One bear at a time was good and easier to manage. They could plan accordingly, and maybe have Meike and Cass snipe them from afar, and leave Teddy and Pickles to deal the final blows.

Pickles paused and scratched at a tree. "We're here. Bear territory."

"How can you tell?"

"Claw marks." He dropped down on all fours and nosed the ground. "And while they're faded, there are bear tracks. And this scent is...this scent is something else." He took one last whiff and turned back to the group, grinning.

They didn't care for that smile one bit.

"Meike, park the mule somewhere safe. Everyone else, draw your weapons! We about to go a huntin' bear!"

21

DON'T HUG ME (I'M SCARED)

Meike never felt quite as vulnerable as they did today, sneaking around the forest for the elusive bear. Speaking in front of a crowd was scary, but knowing there was a ravenous bear just waiting to scoop them up was scarier.

And this wasn't your average picnic eating bear.

They'd instructed Saffron to stay close to the cart, but flee if he had to. There was no guarantee the bears wouldn't target the Rent A Mule and rummage through it for the fresh kills and rations.

"It's fine," Cass said, when Meike raised the issue. "Jasper will sound an alarm if he notices anything." She pointed to the sky, where the bird's silhouette could be seen circling the treetops.

"I hope you're right."

"It's only two bears, and we'll be able to isolate and knock them off one by one. Easier than wasps, too."

"Look at these groves." Pickles nodded at the tree before him. "They made these from the thorns on their backs. See how deep they are?"

Meike squeezed between Teddy and Cass to get a good look. It didn't look like much to them at first, just some scratches in the wood. But the crisscrossing pattern stood out at a second glance.

"It must have a den nearby."

"Exactly! And there's a stream not too far from here. Perfect spot for a bear to bed down for winter."

Someday they hoped to study the natural habitats of the animals and monsters of this world, but that would have to wait. Preferably when they were better outfitted and familiar with the area.

"The tracks lead just into a little grotto. We might catch it while it's resting. Is everyone ready?"

They all answered in the affirmative, with Meike being the only one to hesitate. But it was fine. Pickles, Teddy, Cass...all strong and capable fighters.

"Alright, game plan time! I'm going to sneak up on it. Cass, you hit it with everything you've got, and while it's confused, Teddy can come in and really lay into it. It's not going to know what hit it!"

"What about me? What do I do?"

"Meike, if you see an opening, lob one of those fireballs at it. But try not to hit us."

Easier said than done, but having a plan gave them a much needed boost of confidence.

Pickles rushed out first, the rest of the gang remaining behind, watching as he darted into a cleverly obscured cave. A roar, strong enough to rattle the trees and Meike's eardrums, quickly followed, chasing after the corgi as he barreled out into the open.

A little off script, and the right side of Pickles' head was running red, but he snarled and barked back despite his wounds.

Teddy ran out to meet him, just as the bear revealed itself—or its head, rather.

A great black bear, with hints of purple illuminating its blocky head. It bared its teeth at first Pickles, then Teddy, when goaded. Teddy and Pickles scooted smartly out of the way, allowing Cass to a send a bolt of lightning directly into its snapping jaws.

"Woah," Meike said, but joined in on the chaos with a ball of fire.

The bear, jumping mad and struggling to free itself, could do little to defend itself as Cass showered it with arrows, and Meike threw flame after flame. It slapped most of the arrows away, but retreated from the fire.

"Aw hell," Pickles said, as its head disappeared from view. "I couldn't get the jump on it like I wanted to. You ruin everything, boy."

"Wha—you're blaming me?"

"You came in too soon!"

"I thought you were going to die, old man! I did you a service!"

"Oh quiet, both of you. We have to go after it before it gets away! Don't burrowing animals usually build side exits?"

"Rabbits, foxes, and badgers might," Meike said. "But it's too much of an inconvenience for a bear to bother. I imagine it's not used to running, either."

"Other than the dog, we're all too big to chase after it. But depending on its injuries..."

"Fine," he said, spitting a wad of red tinged saliva onto the ground. "I'll do it. All the fire play must've blinded it, at least."

"You're going in alone? Is that safe?"

Teddy and Cass side-eyed Meike. "Why," Cass said. "Are you volunteering to go with him?"

"...no."

"I'll try one last time to smoke it out," he said, and charged into the cave.

Meike took this moment to replenish their mana stores, already feeling the effects of burnout. It wasn't a great idea to go all out like that, but they wanted to take the bear down quickly and efficiently, making the process as painless as possible—for everyone involved.

"Is it always like this?" And what would they do without Pickles?

"Not usually." Cass edged close to the cave to snag her fallen arrows. "But in cases like these, one would simply wait for the animal to bleed out. It's a pain to retrieve the body, and I've been forced to count it as a loss on more than one occasion."

They couldn't imagine having to climb in after and drag out a full-grown bear. Meike would be happier to take the loss...but the loot!

"Anyway, stay sharp," she said, just as Pickles poked his nose out.

"We're not fully in the clear, but the bear is dead."

"How are we going to get it out?"

"Don't worry about that right now." Pickles disappeared for almost a full minute, reappearing tail first. "Meike, I got a present for ya."

"It's not the bear's heart, is it?"

There was a moment of silence as he exited the hole and tossed a bundle onto the ground. "No, but it's almost as cool as this."

The "bundle" was covered in dense, black fur, gnarled briars sprouting from its back and limbs.

"Pickles! You really did it, you mad lad," Teddy exclaimed, nudging Meike out of the way. "Do you have any idea what it's worth?"

Meike elbowed him away in return to get a better look—and their heart dropped at the realization.

"It's a baby!" Delight and horror fought for Meike's attention, but just looking at that adorable little face melted away any doubts they had.

Meike stared down at the wriggling bundle in their arms. The cub would have years to form its revenge quest if, it decided to carry that grudge into adulthood. But if they trained and treated it right...

The cub was only just forming a series of thorns, more periwinkle than purple.

"And you're just giving it to them," Teddy said, rounding on Pickles.

"Remember dog, I called dibs."

"On the adult bears, not the cub!"

"I'm sure it'll count towards the quest..."

"We are *not* killing it. Or selling it, Teddy! This is the one thing I want, aside from the craftable items and other 'junk'. You all can fight over the rest."

It was risky, giving up whatever loose coin they found along the road, but they were happy to get what they could in rewards. It all added up, really. What Meike couldn't use, they would sell or barter.

"Fine, take it. I don't need any of that junk, but a bear! You could make a small fortune with the right buyer!"

"I don't care. I want a new companion." Much as they loved Saffron, he simply wasn't up to the task.

"There, it's settled. Now, who wants to help me fish out the body?"

Even Pickles, with his obscene strength, couldn't drag out a grown bear on his own. He and the others worked together on excavating mama bear, leaving Meike alone with the latest addition to the party.

"I'm going to call you Alek, short for Aleksei. It means defender."

Little Alek sneezed and pawed at its drippy nose. Yup, it was going to be quite the firecracker once it was grown!

"Shoot, this is going to take a while, isn't it?" Cass guarded the hole alongside Teddy, who was currently yelling back and forth with Pickles. Something about the bear being stuck, Meike gathered.

"What's wrong now?"

"He might be a while, but I don't want to be here for too long."

Meike bounced Alek on their hip. "You aren't suggesting we split the party, are you?"

"I'm not suggesting you tag along, if that's what worries you."

"I hope not," they said. "I'm an important part of the team!"

"You're the designated healer and support." Cass jerked a thumb at the hole. "Pickles is our tank and hard hitter. I'm suggesting you hang back and guard the body and loot while we track down the second bear for the quest."

"So you're just going to leave me alone?" What if the bear found them while the rest of the gang was out?

"It's just a bear, Meike," Teddy said. "It'll be easy for skilled adventurers, such as ourselves!"

"But also, we don't want to risk the cub getting hurt, or someone claiming our loot. Worry not. We'll be swift about it."

In retrospect, Meike could understand why they had to stay behind; one couldn't safely wrangle a bear cub and juggle a fireball at the same time. But being stuck on babysitting duty made them restless. More so when it was just the two of them, and every mysterious sound in the forest sounded like an alarm to them.

Was it approaching danger, or simply a squirrel hunting for nuts?

Meike shrank close to the burrow. If it was big enough for a bear, they could easily squeeze in and hide. Alek pawed at the entrance and whined to be let back in.

"I'm sorry, but this isn't home anymore." But if they were going to be left here for an undetermined time...might as well make the best of it.

They pushed Alek in first and crawled in after him.

Inside, beyond the still cooling body of the mama bear, the burrow widened into a deep groove. Old bones littered the bed of leaves, fur, and sticks. But Meike also found odd items and junk left by previous adventurers, including a boot, a worn scarf, and an old bag with faded lettering.

Nothing worth selling or collecting, in other words.

Alek nudged his mother's body and softly cried for her to wake up and presumably scare away the invader. He did so until he tried himself out and sat down, gazing soundlessly at the ceiling.

"I'm really sorry..." They grabbed the sack and plucked fur from the mother's body. It wasn't much in consolation, but guaranteed her scent would be present and soothe the cub in the meantime.

They easily coaxed him into the bag, where he sat and nibbled on a tuber when Pickles and the others returned—dragging a body far larger than the one trapped underground.

"Found this one terrorizing a family of deer." He spat out thorns and shrugged them off his back. "Now to retrieve the other one."

Other than a clipped ear and drying blood on his flank, Pickles seemed alive and well. Cass and Teddy looked tired. A little dirty, but fine.

"I need a bath," Cass said. "Let's get the cart loaded and take a rest."

Meike, who'd been forced to rest and entertain a restless bear cub, wanted nothing more than to continue on to the next town. But they could use a small nap.

22

ONE NIGHT IN ZACHICK

"Hey. Psst. Hey, kid."

The shady looking man waved at Meike to enter the equally dark and dank alleyway.

Their small group had made it to their destination, Zachick, a bustling hub for traders and adventurers. Meike stayed closed to the Rent A Mule, with Pickles at the rear (something about capping ankles), Teddy covering the front, and Cass on the other side of the body laden cart.

Saffron poked his head from around a bear and quickly retreated as the shady man hissed for Meike's attention.

"No," they snapped, when he inched out of his hidey hole. Meike clutched Aleksei tight to their chest. He was very warm, but too large to hide under their poncho, and had almost wiggled clear of his burlap sack.

"Come on, baby," the man cooed. "I'll give you three hundred for it, whaddya say?"

"Tell him to fuck off," Pickles yelled over the din of the marketplace.

"I'm not saying that! And leave me alone!" They held out a flaming hand, and the man stepped back, hands raised in defeat.

"Just trying to help you out, *damn*."

The group moved through into the heart of the market center, and off-loaded the beasts to be skinned and quartered. Bear meat was considered a delicacy of sorts, whereas the boars were of lesser value.

"I'll leave the boys to guard the cart," Cass said. "Meike, would you like to join me?"

"Sure," they said, bouncing a fussy Alek on their hip. Maybe they could find a harness or leash for the little fella along the way.

Jasper perched on Cass' shoulder, shooting death glares at anyone who dared to stray close to Meike and their cub.

"You handled yourself pretty well back there," she said.

"Thanks? I just didn't want to trade him the bear."

"Good call. Three hundred? Three hundred what, exactly?" She shook her head, clucking her tongue. "He was more likely to rip it from you than give you a single coin."

"I don't care about the money." This bear was their one shot at getting a real battle buddy! He was small and unskilled now, but had great potential.

"Well, you should consider it! If someone makes you a proper offer, you could always use that coin to buy a better pet. Maybe even a mount."

"Aleksei isn't a pet, but he could be a good mount." The cub sneezed into their poncho and rubbed his nose into the mess.

"It's what I would do, anyway. Then again, I have little use for a bear of that age. It's going to take a while for it to mature, you realize that?"

"We'll just have to grow together, won't we, Alek?"

Cass steered Meike towards an extravagant purple tent, manned by a person in hideous yellow fabric and matching hat and boots.

"I've got something for you," she said, handing over the fresh bear pelts.

The man's eyes widened. "Real thorn bear fur! Would you like a pelt?" He glanced over at Alek and frowned. "Can't do much about that one, I'm afraid."

"The cub isn't for sale. I'd like to have the pelts properly tended to. It's for a quest," she added. "We're leaving tomorrow morning, but I won't need them until later this week."

"One of those, eh?"

Cass shrugged. "You know how it goes. Multiple trips simply aren't economical."

"Understood. A week is more than enough time to transform these beauties into a fine coat."

"You do this all the time?"

"I'm a career adventurer. Some people do it just for the money, but for me it's much deeper than that. I specialize in tradeable goods, unlike Teddy."

"I think Teddy does it because it's fun. And Pickles..."

"Is a part-timer. I respect the dog more than the boy, who may well tire of this lifestyle by the time his brain fully matures. Or he gets struck by the lovebug."

Like Anniken...

"Do you run dungeons, too?"

"Only if there's money and loot at stake. But not chump change. I need real stakes, otherwise it's a drag. Gems, gold, that kind of thing."

"Ah..." Meike booped Alek on the nose when he nipped at their sleeve. "I don't know. I think it could be interesting, exploring old caves and fighting kobolds."

"Then have Teddy take you."

They made a quick diversion to a corner of the market filled with cages and kennels. Meike picked out a simple cage, a sling, and a sturdy leash for Alek. Nothing fancy, but it would do for now.

Pickles was nowhere to be found when they returned, leaving only a sour faced Teddy.

"The dog ditched me to go chase skirts! A damned poodle in a tutu. Can you believe that?"

That sounded like Pickles, all right.

"Leave him," Cass said. "Let's get the mule stabled and retire for the night. It's been a long day and I want to freshen up before we ride out at dawn."

"You can retire. I'm going to check the request board. Meike?"

"I need a nap," they said. Cubsitting was hard work.

Getting him into the cage was even harder.

Little Alek fussed and complained, clawing at Meike's hands as they guided him inside. He cried and bit at the bars, but soon tired himself out and settled into a stupor. And Meike slept hard.

"Is that everyone," Cass said, as Meike and their growing collection of familiars shambled into the dining hall.

Meike carried Alek in a sling and led Saffron on a leash. Neither were happy, but at least they were calm.

"We're still waiting on the dog," Teddy said. "Where is that damn mutt?"

"Up yours," came a gruff voice near his kneecaps. "Try looking down for once."

"Okay, now that we're all here..." Cass nodded at Teddy. "Did you find any good quests for us?"

"Several. All local, easy kill and gather quests. Less hogs and bugs, more bears and plants. I even found one that suits you, Meike."

Meike perked up at the sound of their name. "Mushrooms?"

"Aye, you guessed it! But these are no ordinary shrooms."

"Oh..." They were hoping to do some foraging, not killing, but that's just how it goes here.

"Worry not. It'll be as easy as taking candy from a baby." Teddy tried poking Alek's nose and instead came back with a bloody finger. "Little devil..."

"Tell me more about these shrooms..."

"When you whack them, smaller versions come out."

"Like spores?"

"Like spores! But bigger and obnoxious. They're about the size of the cub."

Alek punched his tiny paws into the air.

While they weren't too excited by the prospect of bears, Meike was curious to learn more about the mushrooms. But something else came to mind, something Cass mentioned not too long ago.

"Actually, is it okay if we split up?"

"Why would you want to do something like that?"

Cass leveled her gaze at them. "It would be faster if we fought together, but it wouldn't be wise to bring Alek. Unless you want to use him as bait."

"I don't want him to see bears killed, either."

"Just hang back and cover his eyes," Teddy said, waving a hand through the air. "Me and Pickles can handle it if you and Cass want to tackle the plants and fungi."

Meike's stomach turned. That was the very last thing they wanted! But with a little fire, maybe...

"Right, if that's all."

The Rent-A-Mule was substantially lighter than when they arrived in Zachick. Meike was happy to not have the glazed over eyes of animals staring back at them.

"Okay, the quests call for ten thornback bears, ten man-eating plants, and fifteen fungi."

"That's not so bad."

"We'll take five of the bears and plants, and do the fungi together. How does that sound?"

Cass tapped Meike's shoulder when they raised an objection. "You'll want a full party with those, trust me. They multiply, but the kills only count once."

"Fine." As long as they had a chance to talk.

They splintered off when Pickles found more bear tracks. The plants weren't as straightforward; they blended in a little too well with their surroundings. But bears and giant fungi? How could anyone miss those?

"Ten for you, ten for us," Meike said. Five bears and plants.

"It'll be easy, don't worry." Cass sent Jasper off on a mini expedition of his own, while Meike tried to get a fussy Alek to quiet down. Something about the forest had him on edge.

The first bear wasn't hard to find at all; Meike suspected Pickles sensed it earlier and left it for them to tackle. It was getting a drink from the nearby stream, completely oblivious to the pair of adventurers creeping up on it.

Cass lined up the first shot, a flaming arrow, and sent it flying into the bear's head. It cried out in pain and pawed at its head. Meike followed up with a fire bolt before it had time to process the assault and charge. The mature thorns on its back erupted in flame, and the bear cried out again, throwing itself onto the ground and rolling about to muffle the fire.

Several more arrows thudded into its body, and finally spotting its assailant, the bear snarled and lunged for the cover of the bush.

It jerked in place as an arrow pierced its eye and the skull behind, jaw slacking and body swaying. And then it slumped over with a heavy thud, body lightly smoldering.

Quick, efficient, deadly; that's what Meike liked about Cass. Pickles was more chaotic, plunging himself into the thick of battle. But Cass operated from the shadows, taking down large game before it sensed her coming.

"One down, four more to go." Cass carefully extracted the last of her arrows. "So, what did you want to know?"

"What's an auto-counter?"

"Oh, that old thing." She wiped her hands clean before retrieving a tiny device from her belt. It strongly reminded them of a pager. "It's magitech. Monsters, beasts, and even humans release excess mana when they die. The counter detects this when it's within your vicinity."

"So any death?"

"Not necessarily...I program it beforehand, so it knows which signals to search for. More sophisticated devices relay the information back to the quest giver, but it's so invasive that many adventurers are rightfully wary."

"What's the benefit of having it send the stats for you?"

"Early pay, usually. Or partial, if neither party trust each other. I would only use it for those I've done steady business with. It's just as risky for us. Your reputation is at stake."

"Magitech...how do I get one of those?"

"You need to find a vendor or an alchemist kind enough to make you one." She held the counter between her fingers. "It may not look like much, but it's also an efficient way to restore mana. A weaker potion, if you will. I hear the newer models are better about it, but I don't need anything too fancy."

Meike would be happy just to have a simple model. They weren't planning on undergoing many kill quests, but needed something tangible to keep themself organized.

"Come on, we've barely scratched the surface here! I want to see how you react to the fungi."

"I'm so sorry you had to witness that, Alek."

Meike uncovered his little eyes, but Alek, thinking it was a game, grabbed for their wrists. He was taking it well, at least.

Together, Meike and Cass killed four bears, all males. They were hoping to not come across another mother and cubs.

"Just one bear left," Cass said, looking up from her counter. "And we still need plants...I reckon they don't like communing with natural predators, so they may be a ways off."

"I know they like being surrounded by greenery, like flower fields and dense forests."

"Aye. They tend to stick close to paths and streams, too." She sighed and hugged the freshly killed bear, turning around until her back was firmly pressed into its chest. The massive paws dangled over her shoulders, and the head lolled back at a horrific angle.

Meike tried not to grimace and collected the last of the loot. Mostly a fistful of gold coins, loose fur, and a chipped tooth. They shamelessly pocketed the coins; Cass and the others were going to make a small fortune off selling bear hide and meat. They wouldn't miss twenty gold pieces.

But Meike had a treasure trove of weird and bountiful loot!

Not just the bear fur, money, and Alek, but wasp carapaces, stingers full of venom, herbs, and half-digested meals they still needed to sort through! What the others called "junk" were herbal, maybe even alchemical ingredients.

They could fashion the tooth into a necklace, a gruesome trinket of their labor.

They helped Cass move the bear to the cart, now stacked high with several other bodies. Hopefully they still had room for the fungi, otherwise they'd need to make a quick deposit in Zachick.

"You should take one for yourself. Bear fur keeps you warm in the winter months, especially if you ever travel over yonder."

"I'm fine with wool, thanks." Unlike fur, wool was ethically acquired, and sheep and other woolly animals appreciated being sheared.

Cass grunted, but didn't press further. She led Meike out near a running stream, the quiet side before it turned into a roaring river. Mosquitoes and a heavy cluster of midges hovered over the water, blurring the sky.

They stood back and watched as one tree lunged forward and carved a hole into the mass. More midges quickly flew in to fill the voided space, all too eager to be next on the chopping block.

"Easy pickings," she mouthed, and readied her sword rather than her bow and arrow. The plants weren't so easily felled by any other means—bludgeoning, slicing, and fire was the way to go.

Meike still carried a bit of trauma from their first encounter with the man-eating plants, but recent exposure forced them to adapt. And these things really weren't so scary once you familiarized yourself with their temperament and eating habits.

So while they balanced little Alek and managed blasts of fire, Cass provided support and assailed the monsters up close. Her sword cleaved easily through charred plant matter, though she didn't come out of it entirely unscathed, either..

"Hold on," she said, and downed a minor healing potion.

That was five plants down, and one bear left to go! Either Cass was really strong, or the monsters were just weaker. It gave them a sense of courage, that they could hold up on their own, if needed be. Maybe not against a grown bear, but a flammable plant? Easy!

Meike's bag was now heavy with goods, and would be fuller by the end of the day, thanks to the upcoming shroom harvest.

"Damn it…" Cass bared her teeth and pocketed the counter. "Looks like they took care of the bear for us."

"Oh no," they said, with false disappointment. "Well, time to knock out those fungi!"

"Tch…yeah. By all rights, that last kill should have been ours." More like *hers*, she who collected discarded flesh and hide. "I'll have a talk with the boys later. Let's focus on regrouping. And Meike?"

"Yes?"

"Make sure you're good on mana."

23

WHAT'S YOURS IS MINE

"What did I say, boy?" Cass grabbed Teddy by the collar, not quite shaking or choking him, but coming close.

"Unhand me this instant, woman!" He squirmed in place, but her grip was firm. "And what am I being accused of this time?"

"You know what you did." But she released him with a shove. "Where is it? I want what I am owed!"

"I tried to tell him," Pickles said.

"Et tu, dog? The whole world is against me!" He wailed, flailing his arms through the air.

"Save it for the fungi, kid. Cass, the bear is yours."

"I was going to let her have it! I just...wanted to speed up the process, is all."

"It's been settled, boy. Let's focus on the fungi now."

"Yeah, let's get Meike's stinky boys." Pickles sniffed at Teddy.

"I am not stinky! I bathed...recently."

Cass, Pickles, Meike, and even baby Alek turned their backs to Theodore.

"*Hey*! I have a well-defined musk, but that does not mean I stink!"

The small group made it to what Teddy called "Slime Valley," what looked to be a normal wooded area at first glance. Lots of trees, shrubs, uncomfortably large figures vaguely reminiscent of morels...but not a slime in sight!

"Easy," Pickles said, brushing past their ankles. He was faster on all fours, deadlier on two. But now he approached one shroom and lifted a leg.

"Pickles!"

"It's all good." He sniffed the pee stain left on the shroom. "These guys are docile. They won't hit unless you do."

"Like walking targets, then?"

He curled his lip. "Yeah. It's the friends they drop. Like this..." Pickles took a large bite out of the monster, and it reeled back, thin tendrils appearing and swiping at the source of its displeasure.

Pickles nimbly dodged and hopped onto two feet, one paw reaching around to retrieve his axe. He parried the tendrils with the flat side of his blade. "There!"

A small, pale figure wiggled in the missing space on the shroom's body. It popped out and dove straight for Pickles, who cleaved it in two and flung the remains back at his attacker.

"Cool!"

Cass flicked her sword through the air. "Time consuming, but relatively simple—*Teddy*."

"Your way is less efficient! Try this!" He swung his longsword through the air, clipping four shrooms and leaping back before they exploded by the dozens.

"Damn you, boy! This is their first time!"

"It's okay, Cass. I clean up nicely!" He swung his sword in the opposite direction to catch the hatchlings and deal twice the damage to the originals. "Look sharp, Meike! There's one heading your way!"

"Teddy..." They impaled the shroomling on their sword and awkwardly flicked it away. This wasn't going to be easy with a bear cub in their arms, but there wasn't much choice. "Do you want to go on my back, boy?"

Alek growled in contentment as Meike adjusted the sling so that he was hugging their shoulders. Not ideal, they learned, as he tried to eat their afro before promptly giving up.

Meike danced around Cass and Pickles', staying clear of Teddy's range and aggression. They dealt finishing blows to the shroomlings and got in a good jab or two on the originals.

It was actually kind of...fun? Not that they took enjoyment in killing the poor creatures, but just moving around like this got them almost as hyper as Teddy. They felt *strong*, even. These shrooms multiplied and roved in packs, but their freaky little arms bounced off of Meike's armor, scarcely leaving a mark.

"See? These guys are pushovers!" Teddy lifted one into the air and batted away when it came back in reach.

"You say that now," Cass said, wiping sweat from her brow. "But if you kill enough of these..."

The remaining shrooms fled and swarmed around each other, pressing their bodies tight together, in one massive mound of fleshy bodies and wiggling limbs.

"...they form a mushroom king." She sighed and sheathed her sword. "Oh, what a headache this will be!"

"Oh, Teddy..." Meike didn't terribly mind the monstrous mushroom bouncing in their direction. They had a good team around them.

But...

"You are a truly awful child," Cass snarled. She had her bow primed and at the ready. "I'll deal with you later, but any harm that befalls our healer is on you."

"Me?" Teddy sidestepped the mushroom king and dealt a blow to its side. Dozens of smaller mushrooms toppled out, all reaching for him. "They knew what they signed up for! I'm just giving them the crash course!"

Pickles darted around the stumbling mushroom and spat his axe into his palm. "With all due respect, you're a real pain in the ass, kid." He pivoted sharply and embedded the blade into the belly of the beast. "And that's my role."

"Why is everyone turning on me now? If it were just the three of us, no one would care!"

"I would." Cass peppered the air with a volley of flaming arrows. "I like calculated maneuvers, not utter chaos! Honestly, how did you survive in the mines?"

"Probably cause the kobolds all have two brain cells to rub together. And they all have shit gear." Pickles trampled shroomlings beneath his paws, snapping at those bold enough to touch his muzzle.

Meike imagined little critters running around with rusted swords and cloth armor. Couldn't be any worse than a giant, bouncing shroom that made *boing boooing* sounds each time its body kissed the ground.

"Yeah, yeah, everybody hates Ted! Just help me kill this thing, will ya?"

"Let's just focus on fighting for now," Meike said, as Cass continued to grumble. Yelling at Teddy wasn't going to help or stop him from fooling around.

"Thank you, Meike!"

"Don't thank me." They blasted a smattering of shroomlings with a fireball. There were just so many of them! Only Alek seemed to enjoy himself.

The cub clapped each time a shroom withered away. Were it not for the threat of injuries and even death, Meike might've considered letting him free roam.

Instead, they offered him a half-dead shroom, and he enthusiastically clenched it in his paws. Alek chewed on the poor creature as it shrieked in pain and flailed thin tendrils in the air.

Pickles and Teddy assailed the main shroom with their blades, while Meike and Cass continued to provide support from afar. Wave after wave of shroomlings cascaded from the mushroom king, gradually whittling it down.

Among the loot they collected, Meike found inanimate versions of the mushroom (whether they were edible was up for debate), sticks for kindling, owl pellets, and rocks.

Still, they pocketed it all in hopes of making a tidy profit.

The mushroom king, now more a squire in its current state, flopped over in defeat. The remnants that came crawling out vaguely reminded them of the little demons from an old movie—something about a boy who inadvertently opened the gates of hell in his backyard, and was gifted with an eye in his palm.

Meike waded through the fragile bodies, grimacing with each crunch beneath their feet. "Ugh, gross!" They dragged their soles against the grass to wipe off the gore.

"I'm glad that's your takeaway from all this." Cass sighed and knelt on the ground, a small stack of arrows in front of her. Many were missing their heads, others had broken shafts. "I'm going to need new arrows soon..."

Teddy yawned as he stretched his arms in the air. He dipped into a lunge, bouncing on his heels before changing sides. "That was a great workout! I could really use a nap."

"What you need is a bath," Cass muttered. She took what was salvageable and left the rest to decompose. "Meike, would you like to accompany me to the bathhouse?"

"...bathhouse?"

"It's where dirty boys like Teddy go to wash up."

"Hey!"

"I know what they are," Meike said. "I don't want to...bathe in front of other people."

"Why not? Nudity is natural and nothing to be ashamed of."

"Yeah, I'm always naked!"

"Not helping, dog. Meike, the bathhouses come with special healing properties that not only refresh but strengthen your body and mind."

"Like buffs?"

"If that's what you want to call it, yes. Point being, it's good for the soul. We can request a private room, if you insist."

"When you say we..."

"You, me, the boys..."

Meike ducked behind Cass. "Pickles and Teddy? I can't do that!"

"You've got nothing I want. I only go after furry bitches."

"Pickles."

He winked and stuck out his tongue. "Cassandra."

"We could all use a proper bath, especially you. We need our tank to be at his best."

"Fine, fine, I could use a dip."

"That just leaves Ted—"

"I don't want a bath! Soaking makes my skin all wrinkly and soft!" He moved on from lunges to deep squats. "And besides, it's improper, mixing the sexes."

"Your voice still cracks, Teddy. No one would lust over you, and I'd render you impotent if you tried anything."

"I would never! But if you insist..."

"Very well. I'll secure a room for us."

"Okay mom," he mumbled, and flinched back when Cass fixed her cool gaze on him.

"When this is over, I never want to work with you again. You are an insufferable and reckless child." She strode away, leaving Teddy shaking.

"But we aren't just going to leave now, are we? There's still so much to do!"

"We also have to offload the bodies and turn in quests," Meike said. They personally wouldn't mind retiring from questing for a month or more. They had a lot of loot to sort through.

"Ah...pure bliss." Cass poked her head out of the steaming water, mouth curled into a pleased smile.

That rare smile from Cass left Meike deeply unsettled, but at least she was calm. As were the boys, even Teddy, who proclaimed his distaste for bathing and how it irritated his skin.

And now he was floating on his back in the water, head thrown back and mouth yawned open. Pickles doggy paddled not too far off, occasionally pausing to soak. Meike kept close to the shallow end, wary of passing out from the heat.

They'd left Alek and Saffron in their room for the night, a far more respectable domicile than they were accustomed to. It was nice having money, nicer to be treated with respect and able to afford quality food and lodging.

Cass swam over to them and pressed her back to one of many rocks lining the bath. "Lovely, isn't it?"

"It's alright," they said. Meike rarely had the luxury of a proper bath these days. It was almost cruel to treat them like this. Who knew when they'd next be given the same opportunity?

"Just alright?" She spat out a neat stream of water and squeezed the moisture from her hair. "I'd hoped we could do better than that."

"I meant no offense...I'm just not sure what my reaction is supposed to be?"

"No reaction needed. It's meant to relax and rejuvenate you. Do you think it's working?"

"I guess?" They *did* feel better, but that was only a natural reaction. The warm, salty water soothed every ache and pain and put their body in a state of calm. It would've been better if they were alone, of course. "I feel like I could run a marathon."

"As do I, but save that energy for later." She nodded at the boys. "There's actually something I wanted to talk to you about."

"What about them?"

"Well," she said, lowering her voice, "It's more so about Teddy."

"Oh." They didn't like where this was going, but humored her anyway. "He can be difficult to work with."

"That's very polite of you. But yes, I agree. He's strong, but he's still a child in both body and mind. Pickles is more reliable and has a good head on his shoulders, all things considered."

"What are you proposing?" All this hot air was making their head spin.

"I was going to suggest cutting ties with him, and even Pickles, if need be."

"...what? Why Pickles?"

"He's not like us, Meike."

"Because he's a dog?"

"No, but that's part of it." She allowed her hair to limply hang down to her shoulders. "He's not a proper tank, for one. And there's not much he can teach you, nor do I think him capable of it."

"Teddy I don't mind, but Pickles is—"

She sneered, and it was suddenly the Cass they knew all too well. "You don't honestly consider him a friend, do you? He'd ditch us to chase after girl dogs."

Meike couldn't argue against that. Pickles was fiercely independent and stubborn as a mule. But he was also their mentor, and fun to be around. They'd miss his little antics and knowledge of the world.

"Would you teach me your brand of magic? Archery? Or show me more magitech?"

Her gaze softened. "Yes. I can teach you more than that dog or fool boy can."

"Sure, but what's in it for you?"

"Do you doubt my good will, Meike?"

"No...but I'm tired of being taken for a ride." Patches was one of few people in this world to not trick them so far, to see them as more than an errand boy. Same with Moira...

"I assure you, Meike. I'm not trying to take advantage of you. On the contrary, I'm offering you an opportunity of the lifetime." She rolled her shoulders. "We have great synergy together, and your general disposition doesn't irritate me. I'm not saying it has to be an extensive contract. But just consider it—a month of traveling to put our partnership to the test."

"I don't know...I'd like to keep Pickles." They needed him more as a buffer than anything. Cass was less frightening, now that they'd grown to know her, but she still scared them, particularly when she was scheming.

"You're serious?"

"Pickles is a good boy!" His ears perked up and settled just as quickly. Meike lowered their voice to a whisper. "Just give him a chance."

"Fine. He can continue to play the role of tank, if he so desires. But Teddy is out."

"I..." They glanced at him now, in mid-flip. "Okay."

"Good. Now help me convince the dog."

"Huh?!"

"You're kicking *me* out of the party?"

"All in favor, say 'aye,'" Cass called out. She raised her hand, as did Pickles and an unenthused Meike.

"Come now, this is preposterous! I'd expect this from the dog, of all people, but Meike?" He clasped a hand over his heart. "Et tu? *Et tu, Meike?*"

"Shut up. Shut the fuck up," Jasper cried.

"Silence, Jasper. But yes. We're kicking you out of the party, like one does an unpleasant messenger into the pit of death."

Meike kept their eyes trained to the ground, unable to look Teddy in the eye as two burly men seized him by the arms and hauled him out of the dining hall.

"Damn, you hired goons? That's cold, Cass."

"I didn't want him causing a scene."

An ominous > ***Teddy has left the party*** note hung in the air.

"How'd you do that?"

"Magic," Cass said. "Mythic Script and all that."

"But your hands didn't move!"

"It's magic," Pickles echoed.

"That doesn't..." Meike sighed and rubbed their head. "Whatever. Can we really keep questing with just the three of us? I have a bear cub to tend to, and Teddy was our heavy hitter."

"Not true," Pickles growled. "I'm the heavy. He drew aggro, and I cleaned up."

"We aren't doing anything too strenuous," Cass said. "I don't want to bite off more than I can chew, and I'd rather not carve a path of destruction across the mountainside."

"I want a fourth," Meike said.

"Should we put it to a vote?" Cass' lips trembled. "Though I warn you, the results may not tip so easily in your favor."

"I...Pickles?"

"Doesn't matter to me one way or the other," he said. "I love a good kill quest."

"We can stay on course for the remaining quests, if you'd like. But let's be smart about it."

"Can we at least take time off? I want to craft more potions if it's just going to be the three of us!"

"That's more than fair. Dog, what say you?"

"Sure. We can go over these quests and nix a few. I think the boy just grabbed whatever was available..."

Meike left the two of them to sort it out and returned to their room. It wasn't the mortar and pestle they reached for first, but a roll of parchment and quill pen.

24

SAFE AND SOUND

Achipped tooth and a patch of bear fur rested just above the parchment, silently cheering Meike on as they wrote. Dots of ink stained the corners of the paper and desk.

Dear Patches,

It's been a while since we've seen each other, but you thank you again for supplying me with the spell books! I can cast fireball. >:^)

And make a magic light. I even tamed a few monsters. My latest addition was a bear—the kind with thorns on its back. It's a fearsome little creature! I named him Aleksei. He doubles as both a mount and a battle buddy! I invented that phrase, by the way.

I have a pet rabbit, too, Saffron. He's good for cuddles and companionship, but not much else at the moment. I'm thinking about training him to help with foraging. Since we parted, I've gone on many adventures. I'm very confident about questing now, though I have much to learn. Fire was the first step, but I need to collect the full set of elemental spells. Ice is next on my list, though earth is a close contender.

Again, none of this would've been possible without you. You were the first person in this world to really see the potential in me. I brewed you a few potions to show my appreciation, and included a few trinkets I think you'll enjoy.

Until we meet again,

Meike

The trinkets could be fashioned into a necklace, if so desire.

Meike eyed the note they'd made for themself in the Mythic Script—a list of viable potions they could craft from their current stash. They were eager to try out the stingers in a poison potion, but required a bit of guidance before going on that path. Which is where Moira came in.

Dear Moira,

I've had an excellent series of adventures since I started my travels! But worry not, I am surrounded by excellent companions and have held my own so far. I even subdued a bear and adopted her cub. Everyone insisted I sell it off to someone who might abuse or exploit it, but he's happier with me. I named him Alek!

And I know you're more of an alchemist, but I collected poison stingers from giant wasps. Normally, I'd ask my mentor for help, but she's a very fickle woman. But do you know if the poison is viable? I'm interested in mixing my own poisons. I only have nine of these now;

the tenth is with you.

Unfortunately, I don't know when I'll be back in Lae-
ford. Soon, I hope! I'm excited for you to meet my new
friend and show you all else I've collected. Maybe we
could even manage a stall together, like last time?
Oh, and I fought a Mushroom King. It dropped a
bunch of tiny mushrooms. I don't know if they're edible,
but I'm not bold enough to try them. I included a few
for your inspection.
All the best,
Meike

That said and done, they sealed the letters and prepared to send them off.

"Things are so much easier without the boy, wouldn't you agree?"

"Bigger pockets and less work for us, you mean."

Cass and Pickles were counting out the coin they'd collected from this week's quests. The betrayal of Teddy hadn't stripped him of his share of the pot; Cass allowed him to claim the loot from the Laeford quests, as a sort of compensation for booting him from the party.

Meike took some coins for themself but stacked up on "insignif-icant" loot, more stingers, teeth, claws, a few bones for Alek. They foraged for herbs during travels and replenished their potions at inns and campsites, if the need were dire.

Potion crafting was getting easier and easier by the day, they found; the process was nearly instant now, though the quality was not as standard as the usual method.

"It sure is quieter," they said. "I wonder what he's up to now."

"I'm sure he's fine," Cass said, double checking Pickles' work before doling out the coins—more gold than silver, they were delighted to see. "I like how things are right now, but I wouldn't be opposed to a fourth. We still need a proper tank."

"What about Laken? That knight Anni—Zelamir is dating?"

Cass wrinkled her nose. "A *knight*? I doubt she'd give us the time of day, on top of her usual duties."

"And yet she finds times to chase skirts," Pickles said. He was sneering over his pile of gold. "I doubt the two of them are still together."

"Highly doubtful, indeed. Is this Zelamir a fan of heavy or light armor?"

"She's a fencer...so light." They didn't know what was going on in her love life, and were honestly afraid to ask.

"And is she reliable? Or would I need to leash her, like the boy?"

"Zelamir is a bit like you."

Her eyes narrowed. "So we wouldn't get along, then?"

"No, she's cautious and is more of a leader. She knows how to take charge and treats people fairly."

"Oh, Meike. You don't have to try so hard to flatter me." She sighed and pocketed her share. "There's much I want to teach you, and I may be better able to do so with a reliable fourth, maybe even a fifth."

"Eh, it'll be awhile," Pickles said. "We don't know if she'd even want to come along. Doesn't she have her own band of misfits?"

Meike thought of Casey the Salamander, and that weird goth kid. "Maybe she made some adjustments of her own."

"Look at you, all grown up."

Anniken herself looked worse for wear, one side of her head shaved, the other a mass of loose strands and braids. A heavy black cloak covered her shoulders, obscuring most of her body, but for the leather gloves on her hands and the hint of bracers. A scar graced her cheek, and there were bags under her pale blue eyes.

"I've got a bear," they said, holding up Alek for inspection. The cub had grown a few inches since they first met, and was now almost as big as Pickles. And just as troublesome.

"Indeed." She brushed the bangs from her face. "It's a better battle buddy than that rabbit of yours. Saffron, was it?"

"Saffron never had time to prove himself! But yes...or he will be once he's grown up." They set the cub down and he stood on his hind paws, performing a silly little dance. It was his favorite thing to do these days.

"Cute little fella." She took a long drought from her tankard and set it down with a grimace. "Mind yourself," she said, when he tread over her cloak.

Meike fixed the leash to his harness and gently reeled Alek to rest at their feet. "Sorry, I'm still teaching him his manners."

"How'd you come across a bear cub, anyway? Did you buy him, or..."

"I tamed him! Officially, it's more like adoption."

"I see."

Anniken wasn't back in Laeford, as predicted, but in a town nearly fifty miles away. Pickles called it a waystation, merchant owned and ran, with one large inn to service travelers and adventurers.

"Where's Laken, by the way?"

"Don't know, don't care." She retreated behind her drink. "We're on a break."

"Broke up, she means."

"*Fuck off*, Pickles."

He grinned back at her, tail wagging excessively as he leaned against the table. "Most couples don't recoup their losses."

She glared at him and turned to Cass. "I don't know how you manage with that mangy mutt."

"Oh, me and Pickles have our differences, but we're able to set those aside for the sake of a common goal. Isn't that right, Meike?"

"If you say so," they mumbled. "I'm sorry about...her."

"I really don't want to talk about it right now."

"Her pride's wounded."

"*I said not now, Pickles.*" She didn't look so tired now, at least. "I don't mind joining you. Things fell apart with my old crew after...the incident with Laken. Tried going solo for a while, but it's not as easy as it seems."

"What happened?"

"I tried to take on too much, and it all caught up with me."

"Ah, burnout," Cass said. "I prefer soloing as well, though I'm not at my limit yet."

"I need a change of pace, is all. I don't mind leading or striking out on my own, but..."

Pickles was suspiciously quiet for once, so it was Meike who broke the silence.

"We should take turns! Like a democracy."

"Yeah, why don't you take the lead, Meike?"

They flicked him on the nose, and he let out a sharp bark. "I was going to nominate Cass. She's been the closest thing we've had to a leader."

"If you insist—"

Everyone but Cass raised their hands.

Cass sighed and crossed her arms, upsetting the bird on her shoulder. "It's going to be like that, then? Just don't expect me to command your every step. I'm not a tactician." Her eyes glinted as she glanced at Meike. "That's a role better suited for your position."

"Me? I'm just support."

"She's right," Anniken said. "You don't have to lead, but you can give out suggestions on the battlefield. For raids and dungeons, you'll want more organization and defined roles. You're all just winging it right now, aren't you?"

"Meike for sure," Pickles said. "I have my own plan in mind."

"We're all winging it," Cass said. "But we all work well together."

"Good. I don't want to commit to anything right now, but I'm fine with a trial run." She tugged on Meike's poncho when they stood up. "Glad to see you're still running around in this. I can make you something better, if you like. Your armor could use some touching up, too."

"You don't have to do that!" Although, the poncho was getting shabbier and shabbier by the day. Meike tried to take care of it, but the quality wasn't the best to start. "And I can always commission new armor when I need it. I'm always in the back, so I don't get hurt much."

"Better to be safe than sorry." She dropped her hand. "I still have the same sword, but I upgraded everything else. A good sword will last you awhile, but armor wears down faster. I'd like a new sword and some sturdy boots—there's a tailor that adds enchantments for an extra fee."

"What, like jumping boots?"

"Agility enhancements! I can do acrobatics on my own, but nothing close to what xe is proposing."

Was that a neopronoun? "I want to meet xem."

"Oh, right...you're nonbinary too." She chewed on her lip. "I keep collecting people like you. Almost makes me wonder."

"Who are the others?"

Anniken slowly shook her head, retreating from the inquiry. "Xe is a bigger loner than you, so don't get too excited. Xe live out in the sticks, but occasionally stops by Zachick to tend to the shop. I can give you the coordinates later."

"Do you want to scout out the quest board now, or should we wait?" They wanted to meet this magical person soon.

"Sure," Anniken said, fishing out a small device from her utility belt.

"What is that?"

"This?" She held up what looked to be a PDA. "Laken got it for me before we..." She sighed and curled her hand around it. "They're supposed to be really hard to come across, so I can't blame you for not knowing. But it's like a tiny computer."

"*What*?" They turned to Cass, who seemed unfazed. "Did you know about this?"

"Yes, but I can count the number of connections I have on one hand, and certainly no one I couldn't reach with a pigeon."

"It's an auto-counter, a communications device, and it allows me to browse requests near and far. I couldn't live without it," Anniken said, smiling as if she were posing for an ad.

"Pickles! Did you know about this?"

"Yeah? I don't use an auto-counter, either." He rolled his eyes. "Technology makes you soft and reliant."

"Technology makes life easier by eliminating tedious tasks," Anniken said, tapping away.

Meike stared in disbelief. They learned something new every day, light years behind everyone else. "Find a good quest. I need...money!"

25

AMATEUR ARBORIST

"Woah, is this your mount?"

Anniken nodded at the magnificent horse. It had a cream-colored coat, brown legs and mane. And the long, pointy horn of a narwhal.

"Is it a unicorn?" Meike stood a safe distance from the creature, mindful of its reach.

"Not quite. Vallens is just a horse with a horn."

Vallens snorted and tossed his mane.

"Sorry, boy. It's easier this way." He only settled down when she rubbed his head. "Vallens was a gift…"

"From Laken?"

Anniken winced. "That name again. This was her way of getting me to stay. Ironic, don't you think?"

They set an antsy Alek by their feet, secured by his harness and leash. "What happened?"

"Laken's a notorious flirt," she said, pulling her teeth back in a snarl. "I love her, but…" She shook her head. "And so we're on a break."

It didn't make any sense to Meike; why not end it? If there was no trust, what was the point?

"Don't give me that look. You've never been in love, have you?"

"Nope."

"Count yourself lucky." She sneered and stepped back. "Don't mention her name to me again, understand?"

Meike nodded, left with the impression that love wasn't worth its price in salt.

Pickles and Cass idled nearby, talking in quiet tones as they prepared the mule for the next round of adventures.

"Get on," Anniken said, from the back of her mount.

"You want me to ride with you?" What about the others?

"Or would you prefer to ride in the cart?"

It didn't matter either way to Meike; they liked being able to hop in and out with ease, and grab some extra materials. But how often did they get to ride a horse?

Anniken helped them on the horse, but try as they might, Meike could not find a comfortable position. Presumably this was something that got better with time.

"It's faster this way, trust me." She pressed her heels into the horse's sides, and it took off at a steady trot.

The mule followed just a step slower, its cart lighter with just Cass and Pickles in the back. Little Alek and Saffron rode in the deepest part, the former curled up and napping in the sack found in his old den.

"You need to secure a mount of your own, at least until that cub is old enough. Even then, a proper horse will do you well. Rent one if you have to."

"I don't think that's necessary right now."

"It's faster," she insisted. "The mule slows us down, but it's convenient for carrying loot and our gear."

Meike had a feeling Anniken had no need for cargo haulers, that she was more discerning about the loot she collected and the battles she fought. Both like and unlike Teddy.

"I'll look into it," they said, and the conversation died there.

There were some pretty good quests to be found at the waystation, though Anniken suggested two at the most. One was a simple "kill x amount of monsters" quest, the other was gathering; chopping wood from magical trees.

"We only have so much space," Anniken said, eying the cart. "How do you want to do this?"

"I'd rather do the hard work first," Cass said. "Killing wolves is always a hassle, but should go quickly if they come at us in pairs."

"And I'm game for whatever," Pickles said. "Meike?"

"I think we can save the logging for after. It'll be relaxing." The quest didn't say they had to fell every tree; there were bound to be some lying about, just ready for the picking.

Anniken snorted. "If you say so."

"Why do you say it like that?"

"Where do you think the wood is coming from?"

Meike froze. It felt like a rhetorical question, but... "Trees?"

"Trees, they say! Not just trees, Meike. But *treants*."

"We're killing tree *people*?" Their stomach dropped. "But the quest didn't say anything about killing trees! Just chopping."

"Oh, bless your heart," Cass said. "No, we aren't hunting the mature ones. Only saplings."

"We're killing their *children*?"

"Well, not necessarily. They'll grow back."

"Sure, their bodies may regenerate, but not their individuality!" Meike groaned and buried their face in their hands. They thought this cycle of their life was over after what happened to Alek's mom. Or the sow...

"It's just trees, Meike. Monster trees."

"I don't want to kill their saplings!"

"Here's a thought," Anniken said. "Why don't we target the mature trees? We'd actually save time. The older ones are essentially walking logs."

"Yes please," Meike said, before anyone could voice dissent.

Days like this made them want to retire to a cozy workshop and spend their days crafting potions and harvesting ingredients from their garden. That desire came often these days...

"Don't know what's got you all worried," Cass said, waving Meike away from the cart. Freshly killed wolves laid in the back, in a neat stack to accommodate the logs. "You did well."

"Only with your help." Didn't even need to draw their sword.

"I debated on giving you the crash course during, but—"

"And what are you two whispering about?" Anniken's silhouette came into view.

"Just taking a breather," Cass said, rolling her shoulders.

Her eyes narrowed. "And how is the hunt?"

"We're down to one wolf. You?"

Anniken hoisted one of many kills into the cart. "All done. Pickles is coming with the last of them."

"Nice!" Anniken's efficiency had a trickle down effect. Meike hoped to match that someday, to be an inspiration to their carries.

"Don't get too excited. We still need to tackle those trees."

Their stomach fell, but Meike kept up a brave face. "I've made my peace with that."

"Now then, this is a good time for a quick lesson in elemental magic."

"Meike knows fire, don't you?"

"Let me finish, please." There was an edge in Cass' voice. "This is the sort that centers around enchantments. Or flaming swords and arrows, if you want the simple version."

"Oh sweet! I've been dying to learn that trick." They were practically vibrating in place.

"Now, take out your sword, and imagine you're forming a fiery orb from your hand."

"So like usual, then?" Meike pictured it in their mind and slowly pushed that energy forward. The flame formed first around their fist, and gradually strained upwards along the edge of the blade. "Am I doing this right?"

Cass sighed. "Not entirely, but it's a good start."

They gingerly waved the sword around and watched in awe as the flame remained constant, flickering only at the very edges. "Oh, this is so cool!"

"You should have a staff or grimoire commissioned. Or both. I know some mages use wands as well, but they aren't nearly as potent as the other conductors. Plus, you get to slap people with a book! Imagine how fun that could be." Cass chuckled and crossed her arms. "That's what I would do, anyway."

"Get one of those iron staffs so you can do stabbing damage," Anniken said, with too much enthusiasm for Meike's tastes.

"I think I'd be fine with a grimoire. Who can make one for me?"

"A scribe," Cass said, while a disgruntled Anniken wandered off. "You won't find them at the waystation or any of these smaller towns, but in cities. Laeford and maybe even Zachick."

"I'll look around Laeford. I'm already familiar with the city, and I have friends there." They tripped over the word; Moira wasn't an acquaintance, but she wasn't quite a friend, either.

"You do that. Look lively, now."

They stepped aside to let Pickles and Anniken come through. "Annoying whelps," he said, snarling around the haunches of a wolf. "One of them got me, Meike. I need healing."

"Sure!" At first glance, he seemed fine, but they spotted a slowly bleeding gash on his right side. "Do you want to rest for an hour before we continue?"

"Don't baby me," he snapped, but settled down when Meike offered a potion. "But I guess I could catch my breath while y'all take care of that tenth wolf." Pickles climbed into the cart and curled up among the wolves. Little baby Alek sat in a basket in the far back, watching with curious eyes.

"Okay. Anniken?"

"You don't need me to take care of one little wolf." She flicked the tip of their sword. "Break that in, why don't you?"

"If you say so..." Meike performed a few more practice swings and chopped into the underbrush, leaving steaming plant matter in its wake. "This is going to hurt, isn't it?"

"Possibly, if you move like that. Do you want me to teach you the proper way?"

"I know how to use a sword!" They swiped it through the air and it whooshed and whistled.

"Okay, that's a step up from before! But your form is all wrong..."

"Anniken." They held the sword out of her grasp. "I know how."

"Fine. Bring the wolf back without singeing its fur. Otherwise I will instruct you."

In some ways, she was worse than Teddy.

The soft chatter of their associates died down as Meike trekked into the woods. They didn't have a game plan in mind; winging it hadn't failed them so far.

Meike employed strategies learned from their travels. Their eyes weren't as keen as Pickles, but they knew to search the ground for tracks, and the trees and underbrush for signs of disturbance.

"Please don't make this harder than it has to be," they whispered, sword at the ready. It dimly glowed, radiating warmth and illuminating the area.

Meike slowly rotated the sword, using the lighting to their advantage. There...it was faint, but the shadow of a paw stood out among the dirt and leaves.

They nudged the debris away from the mark and followed its trajectory to more up ahead. Prints marred by uneven footing and drips of crimson.

One good blow and the deed was done.

Meike had their sword at the ready when a furry figure came into view. It was smaller than your average wolf, with shaggy gray fur and strained movements.

A branch cracked under their foot, and the wolf turned with a growl. It crouched low to the ground, teeth bared.

"Hold on, I'm not going to hurt you," they said, putting the sword away. "I think we could help each other."

Again, the wolf growled, but it made no move away from or towards them. This was an easy kill, and depending on the severity of its injuries, grounds for a mercy kill.

Instead, Meike reached for a flask of water. The wolf inched away, a nasty snarl building in its throat.

"I'm just trying to help. If I wanted to kill you, I would've done so." They had something grander in mind, instead.

It huffed but remained stationary, watching as Meike approached.

"Here." They poured water over the wounds, washing away drying blood and dirt, followed by a minor healing potion.

The wolf flinched back with a whimper, but Meike persisted until the beaker was empty. And then watched in awe as flesh knitted itself together, and fur receded to cover the healed flesh.

"Magic is beautiful," they whispered.

The wolf licked excess fluid from its side and sat up, gazing at its mender with curiosity.

"Anniken won't like this, but do you want to join us?"

"Oh Meike," Anniken said, shaking her head in disapproval. "What have you done now?"

"I adopted a wolf!" Meike gestured to their new friend, who "smiled" back at Anniken. "I'm not entirely sure what gender it is but—"

Pickles circled the wolf, his nose twitching. "It's female," he said.

The wolf snarled and bared her fangs at him, and Pickles responded in kind.

"That explains why it's so small," Cass said, watching from afar. "Are you sure you'll be able to tame it?"

"She's tame! She likes me." They carefully extended a hand to the wolf. "Isn't that right...Vivica?"

"You named the wolf Vivica?"

"Or Vee, for short. It's a good name."

Anniken stood just behind them, inspecting the wolf. "She might be easier to handle than a male. Just have to keep an eye on Pickles."

"Oi! She's not even my type!"

"And I suppose Vee could snap your back in a second, if she really wanted to." Anniken reached for the wolf but retreated when she growled. "Right, no pets. But what are you going to do with all these animals?"

A rabbit, a bear cub, and now a wolf...

"She can walk alongside us," they said. "I don't want her near Saffron or Alek."

"That's smart. We might have use for her in battle."

"Maybe later. She's still recovering from her wounds. And I'd rather not have her fight against her old allies."

"Oh, the tenth wolf? No need." Anniken jerked a thumb at the cart. "I hunted it down while you were out making friends."

"Thanks..." Well, that was one less thing to worry about! "Are we moving on or resting for the night?"

"Rest," Cass said. "The next step is logging, and I want to be well rested before I go and throw my back out."

"Come on, girl," Meike said, patting her on the back. "Let's get you settled!"

She still needed some coaxing, but Vivica settled down into a light doze outside the tent. Saffron, understandably, refused to budge from the safety of the cart, but Alek was happy to wander around on his stubby little legs.

"I can't believe you tamed another animal," Cass said, watching the wolf with awe. "Perhaps you've found your true calling, Meike!"

The four of them sat around a low cooking fire. The plan was to sleep in cycles, with one person standing watch. Meike was happy to take first watch, Cass second, Anniken third, and Pickles last.

For now, a light dinner and heals were in order.

Meike turned down the roasted wolf meat for a meal of mushrooms, berries, and an assortment of herbs foraged from the forest. They couldn't say no to the loot, a mix of fangs and claws.

"What makes these trees so special? What is their lumber used for?" Wands and staff came to mind, but wouldn't it be simpler to just harvest branches and fallen logs instead?

"Many things, including musical instruments," Cass said. "I hear a famous conductor had a player piano made from such wood."

"And lesser known magical catalysts," Anniken said. "Such as talismans and wooden companions. Like puppets."

Horrific animatronics came to mind. "Anything an alchemist could use?" Like Moira, maybe. Surely she could benefit from a goat constricting cage.

"What are you thinking about?"

"I don't know yet." They would have to run this by Moira or the quest giver. There surely had to be a more efficient way of managing their growing collection of battle buddies.

"Regardless," Cass said, "I recommend taking some wood for yourself. Commission something nice for yourself. It's not exactly top tier, but the wood is still worth its price in salt. I, for one, would love more arrows."

"Arrows?" Anniken looked puzzled for once, Meike was excited to see. Normally they were the one in left in the dark.

"Magical conductors. I'm skilled with both bows and the arcane. They make for excellent bedfellows."

"I'd like something like that, but with swords and daggers."

"I can teach you." She smiled, eyes flickering in Meike's direction. "I already offered my assistance once. I don't mind sharing it further."

"Do you know how to use magic, Anniken?" A hint of smugness leaked into their tone.

"I know enough. I can summon magic lights and make little fires."

"You'll need a bit more than that," Cass said, "but you're on the right track."

"Aye." She sipped from her canteen. "I'm heading off to bed, you?"

"I think I'll stay up just a while longer, if that's alright with Meike."

"I don't mind," they said. The company was much appreciated.

Pickles grunted and wiggled under a bed of leaves. "Just keep it down, will ya? We've got a big day ahead of us."

The trees were all a shade of deep purple and dimly glowed in the low light. Contrast that with the vivid forestry around it—the intense green of the grass, the clear blue sky, the many bugs and critters in various colors. They even spotted a giant, multi-colored squirrel that would be right at home in India; it was blue and red with golden paws and belly.

Meike leaned on their axe, admiring the tree before them. Somehow, they'd been convinced to target the still living trees. The catch?

"Just get on with it, dog," Anniken whispered. "Before the trees wake up." She drove her axe into hers and gave it one good kick, toppling it over.

"Can't you hear them crying?" A shiver ran down Meike's spine. Surely Pickles heard, with his sharp doggie ears. But he only whacked his tree again and again, the shrill cries assailing Meike's ears with each blow.

"I hear them," Cass said, in a whisper so soft it might as well have been the wind. "Gods, I hear them. Let's be quick about it, shall we?"

Meike lifted their axe as Vivica growled and skulked closer to the cart, where the small familiars hid.

They didn't understand what, exactly, but Cass put a spell over the trees to inhibit movement and minimize aggression. But the magic was on a short timer, no longer than thirty minutes.

Anniken rolled her fallen tree to the side and moved on to the next one. By comparison, it took Meike five minutes to fell one tree. And by then, Anniken had three under her belt.

If this were a game, Pickle would be winning. He had six sizable logs under his belt, felling one after another with one or two good whacks. He was awfully strong for such a small dog.

By the end, Meike had three logs, Cass six, Anniken twelve, and Pickles, a whopping twenty six.

"Pickles! What did you do?"

"Huh, almost fifty...I did my job," he snarled, when Meike poked him with their axe. "I got your damn logs."

"You chopped down too many!"

"That I did." He rolled over on the lush grass, kicking his paws in the air. "Was a good day. I'm all tuckered out."

"Don't get too comfortable." Anniken nudged him with her foot. "We've got less than four minutes before these trees wake up and start calling for our blood."

"Four minutes..." Meike stared dismally at the amount of logs piled up. There was no way...

"Leave the logs to me." He stretched out on his belly, tail wiggling in the air. "Just watch my back."

They all scrambled to collect the logs, There was simply no way they could collect all of them before the trees roused. In fact, only six logs were loaded when the first tree uprooted itself.

Vivica crept from her hiding space and brushed against Meike. "Vee!"

But the wolf slammed her body into the outstretched claw meant for Meike. VIvica sank her teeth into the tree's arm and jerked her head from side to side, resulting in an unpleasant groaning.

The tree uttered a thin cry as its arm was torn from its body. It flailed with its one remaining arm, but Vivica sprang out of reach.

"Good girl," Meike said, as she continued to get the best of the tree. But there was only one of her, and an infinite amount of trees.

"Leave her," Pickles snapped. "Mind the logs!"

Together, Pickles and Vivica fended off the monsters while Meike and the others scrambled to fill the cart. It was very touch and go at certain points, with the clear target being the fallen comrades.

Meike was forced to scorch several trees to secure their goods. "Sorry! I really am!" But it simply couldn't be helped.

"Are we good," Pickles called over the din.

"We still have..." Meike gave the pile a quick scan. "Twenty five logs to go!"

"Oh, no we don't. Twenty two is plenty!" He knocked back a persistent claw from Anniken's cloak. "Let's bail!"

Meike couldn't argue against that. They darted between two encroaching trees, branches curved into massive claws, and scrambled into the cart as Cass kicked it into gear.

Anniken's horse kicked a tree blocking the path, and then they were off.

26

SPELLBOUND

"It's a shame we couldn't grab the others," Anniken said, peering into the cart. Between the logs and the piled up bodies, it was quite the sight.

Vivica watched Alek with wary eyes from her spot under a berry laden bush. All poisonous, by Meike's guess; the red hue of the berries and the prickly thorns surrounding them weren't promising.

"You should take the extra two," she continued. "Make you a nice staff or even a wand! There's plenty of sticks back here…"

"I think I'd rather have a grimoire than a wand." A staff and a grimoire, both good choices! "It's what I always looked for in a class."

"Are you still treating this like a video game?" She sighed and hopped out of the cart. "You need to move on from that."

"And get into the real world," they said in a mocking tone. "I know, but I want to be comfortable, too. I want to be my authentic self."

Back in the "real world," Meike had to abide by rules they didn't fully understand, unspoken rules even their neurotypical peers didn't hold to. They were expected to go to school, find a career, and while their parents gave up on pushing that narrative, marry and have kids.

Boring, boring, boring!

They didn't care about dating or marriage or children. Forestry, mushrooms, and the mysterious healing element of plants mattered to them the most. Working at the farm was just one step towards their coveted master's degree, and following that, years of research and days spent under the sun or poring over notes, tea cups, and telescopes. Their hobbies would be there for them when work and life grew too much to bear.

"What's your secret, Annie?" There was no point in keeping up with aliases when it was just the two of them; Pickles and Cass were doing their own thing.

"I don't know what you mean."

"What's your endgame? I know what I want, but what about you?"

"Don't know," she said, after a moment. "I'd like to keep traveling and see what all this world has to offer."

"And Laken?"

"It's complicated." She snapped off a branch and twirled it between her fingers. "I still love her, but I wonder..." The branch cracked in her hands. "It's entirely up to her, but I want to focus on myself for now." She tossed the remnants away and dusted her hands off. "And get stronger, strong enough to best her in a fight."

Meike tilted their head to the side. "Why a fight?"

"So she'll take me seriously and see just how devoted I am to her. Don't you understand how romance works?"

"No." Fighting was...romantic? Did Anniken take lessons from Tamanegi-sensei?

She sighed and leaned against the cart. "No, I suppose you wouldn't."

Cass returned half an hour later, alone. "Looks like I beat the dog," she said, and held up her arm in triumph. "I caught us dinner."

Hanging from a strap were the corpses of three plump rabbits. "One for each of us, though I fully suggest saving some for the nights ahead."

"Do you need help," Anniken said.

"That would be grand, thank you. It'll go faster with the two or...three of us." She winked at Meike.

"I don't mind helping!" And they rather liked her now. "Just as soon as I put this guy down for a nap."

Alek was dying to run free, and Meike obliged—although they kept him leashed with some slack. With nothing else to do, he would eventually tire himself out and curl up to sleep.

With Cass and Anniken on either side, Meike sat down to dissect and clean their rabbit. It was a pretty buck with chestnut colored fur. They showed Anniken how to skin it and offered it to her for future tailoring.

"I'm surprised you know how to do this," she said. "I thought you were a vegetarian."

"I am! Pickles taught me. While I don't eat the meat, I can still sell or give it to someone in need."

"How kind of you." She grimaced at the inelegant cut she made, but the fur was mostly intact. "Do you know how to cook them, too?"

"No, but Cass does." Meike had a rough idea of how to do so, should it ever come to that. But they lacked the will.

"How'd you feed yourself, Zelamir?" Her mouth didn't twitch, but Cass' voice carried a tone of amusement. "It's a necessary life skill."

"A good supply of rations, mostly. My old party had a skilled chef, so we were never hurting for food."

"Does hand crafted food contain stat bonuses, too?" If it worked for the hot springs...

"Yes," Cass said. "The quality depends on the chef's expertise, of course. I'm on the lesser end of that, myself."

"You know so much!" From archery to magic, and now magical cooking?

Cass chuckled to herself. "You're easily amused, aren't you? I could teach you a bit, in theory. As an herbalist, you have a bit of an advantage already. Have you tried making tea?"

"I did once," they said, recalling that little prank Maggie pulled. "I didn't think much of it at the time."

"You should give it some serious consideration, my dear! I recommend making your own tea leaves, if possible. You're the forager, after all."

"Magic tea!" They didn't have all the needed materials at the moment, but perhaps when they stopped in town...

"Who's making tea?" A blur of orange fur darted into view. Pickles' fur was damp from his little dip in the spring. He shook himself one last time, a safe distance from the others, before joining them. "It's been so long since I last had a good cuppa!"

"And it'll be quite some time still," Cass said, poking him on the nose when he sniffed at the carcass of her neatly dressed rabbit. "Do us a favor and get the fire going."

"Y'all can go shopping," Pickles said, curling up by the inn's large fireplace. "I'm going to help myself to belly rubs and scraps."

"You too, dog," Anniken said, reaching for his scruff.

He snarled and snapped at her fingers, the same hand he bit during their first encounter. "Do you want to lose the rest?"

"Just try it." She dug her hand into his fur, and Pickles bit into the protective armor securing her arm. There was no doubt in Meike's mind that he would rip through the leather to the soft flesh below.

"Enough, both of you," Cass called clear across the room, startling the trio and other travelers.

Pickles' jaw went slack, but he didn't immediately back down.

"You too, Zelamir."

"He's being entirely unreasonable!" But she released him. "You can't keep running into battle with that old battered axe! You need a better weapon, maybe even armor."

"There's nothing wrong with my gear, just like there's nothing wrong with my bite." He snarled, fur bristling.

"I said enough. You can't force the issue, and Pickles hasn't failed us yet."

"You tell her, sister."

"Don't give me that. You can, at the very least, have your axe sharpened. It's looking a little dull."

Pickles yawned and rolled onto his back, idly pawing the air. "Won't take five minutes!"

"Only if you arrive early, and not a moment longer. You can spend the rest of the day snoozing, but I advise not waiting until lunch." She lowered her voice, adapting a conspiratorial tone. "I hear the cook likes to feed the strays, but you may be able to catch her before that."

One of his floppy ears stood to attention, and Pickles eyed Cass with something close to respect. "I like you more than the white one." He groaned and hopped onto his feet. "Alright, let's get to it!"

"Is that really all it takes?" Anniken looked unhappy about the whole thing, but she fell in line as the group left the inn to the foggy town awaiting them.

Zachick was far less crowded in the morning than it was at the height of day, when vendors and shoppers alike were beating the lunch rush and trying to catch the best deals. Pickles and Anniken left the group first to have their weapons tended to.

Meike closely followed Cass to help drop off the quest items—mostly the logs and wolves, the latter of which were to be skinned and their meat salvaged. It was hard to believe anyone would want to eat wolf; the meat couldn't be that good. But Cass assured them that there was a market for it, just as there was a market for their fur.

"Are you sure you don't want a new coat?"

They thought of poor Vee, locked in a pen outside of the inn. Meike could safely smuggle in their rabbit and cub, but the innkeeper refused to allow "wild animals" on the premise. Anniken tried arguing that Pickles was a far greater threat, but he easily won over the innkeeper with the saddest little whine and puppy dog eyes.

"What I have is enough."

"You don't know that. What if we decide to go into the mountains? That little cloak won't keep you warm."

"But I don't want to wear a dead animal's skin, either!"

Cass rolled her eyes. "Keyword here being dead. Of which you had a hand in, need I remind you?"

"Yeah, but—"

"No buts. I won't have you dying from frost on my watch, under-stand?"

"Understand," Jasper repeated.

"Alright."

"Good! Now, how about we get you that staff?"

"Would you prefer a one handed or full staff," the stern faced man said, peering at Meike from his side of the counter. He had patchy facial hair and looked to be around Cass' age.

"A full staff, please."

The man—Rickard—made a note on the order sheet. "Stand in front of the board, please."

The board reminded Meike of those measurement charts one might find in a doctor's office. They did as instructed, placing their back to the board, and resisted the urge to wiggle as Rickard measured them.

"Does it matter how tall I am?"

"Quite a good deal, actually," he said, making a spot just above their head. "As does your intention. A staff can be a magical conductor, or a simple offensive weapon."

"Oh, like martial arts?"

His eye twitched. "Something like that. Size also matters in that I don't want to give you a weapon too long or short for practical use. Taller users can benefit from longer staffs, but it's not a hard and fast rule. Someone smaller and nimble would prefer something that matches their personality."

"Are you implying short people have bigger personalities?" Because Meike's always felt diminished.

"Mayhap." He tapped them on the shoulder. "Now, the wood you've given me is simply exquisite. Second only to—"

Cass cleared her throat. "We don't have all day, Rick."

He wiped his brow with a handkerchief. "I don't do rush jobs, no matter the cost. I can have this formed and ready by next week."

"A week?" Meike's voice sounded squeaky in their ears. "I don't know if we can stay here that long!"

"It's fine," Cass said, patting their shoulder. "Rickard is a professional, and you can't rush art. However, I think it would be pertinent for him to focus on the cages."

Rickard perked up. "Are you an amateur summoner?"

"They're a monster tamer. I suppose someday Meike could learn summoning magic, but not anytime soon."

"Forget the cages," he said. "No, with this kind of wood—"

"Rickard."

He bowed his head. "Apologies. But I can make you something of better quality—and style." He winked. "But first, I'm going to need a list of the critters young Meike here keeps."

"A rabbit, a wolf, and a bear cub," they said.

"Ooh, interesting collection! I'm going to have fun with this. And don't worry, I'll find a use for the remainder."

"I promise you won't be disappointed," Cass said, when Rickard's stall was behind them. "He's quite the loquacious chap, but very good of heart." She sighed to herself. "And me and him are alike in many ways, while being vastly different in others."

"You're speaking in riddles again."

Cass smiled at them. "We have more in common than you know." But she didn't elaborate. "Here, you'll find your future grimoire."

She'd led them to a stall obscured by a thin black curtain. Parchment and leather bound books lined the stable and shelves, and standing in the middle, blending in perfectly with the shadows, was a heavily cloaked figure. Striking green eyes stared back, beckoning them to speak.

Meike offered a timid, "Hello."

The figure nodded. "How may I help you?" Their voice was soft, like pages of freshly printed paper dancing in the wind.

"I'm an aspiring mage, in desperate need of a grimoire. Can you help me?"

"An aspiring mage?"

"Y-yes. I can perform some magic."

"But then you are a mage, and not a mere pretender!" They chuckled quietly to themself. "Take a look at my wares and let me know which strikes your fancy."

"Are the books pre-enchanted?" Meike glanced at the rows of colorful and ornate books. Doubtful magic books would be left to sit so freely.

"No, these are but mere husks. I'll personally enchant and outline them with skills of your preference. For a price, of course."

Meike's coin purse begged for them to take it easy. "Can I request a custom design?"

"Of course! What do you have in mind?"

"I want something forest related, like trees, streams, woodland critters..."

The bookseller blinked slowly, like a cat. "I have something like that available. 'Rabbits At Play,' is what I call it."

"I don't need to see it to know it's amazing! I'll take it, please."

"Excellent choice, my child."

"Can you give me a list of spells and prices to choose from? I'd like to come back for it by next week, but I can give you a deposit for now." If they were paying per spell, Meike wanted to be prepared.

"You and I are going to be good friends..."

"Meike!"

"Yes, Meike. And you can call me Joie."

27

ALL TAPPED OUT

Meike's venture into the marketplace didn't end with Joie. Cass insisted they both have their weapons sharpened, and they were glad for it. Having a freshly honed sword and knife was oddly satisfying, even if they mainly used the knife for clipping mushrooms.

"Now, how do you intend to spend the rest of your day," Cass said, having finished admiring the new heads on her arrows.

"I still need to pick out some spells..." A quick glance told them that these wouldn't come cheap. Most were fifty silver, while some went as high as ten gold coins! Daunting, but great power was at their fingertips!

But they still had the staff and side pieces to consider...

Meike sighed, feeling the weight of the world on their shoulders. "I need to make some fast money."

"You can start by selling some of that junk. And you have herbs, don't you?"

"I do...we've got a week, so why waste it?"

"And while you do that, I'm going to have a look around, maybe have a soak. We all could benefit from a bath."

"Don't worry about me," they said, and went off in the opposite direction.

Meike had at least forty gold pieces bouncing around in their coin purse, or fifteen if you counted their current expenses. They still had some silver, but not enough to convert into gold.

They locked themself in their room for a good two hours, sorting through the accumulated loot. Most of it was pure junk—bear fur, fangs, wasp carapaces, plant matter, half-digested meals, over forty pieces of mushrooms—and stingers oozing with poison. The stingers weren't for sale.

They tossed the junk back into their bag, but left the healing herbs out and stingers out.

Whipping up the healing potions was a simple affair for the well-trained Meike, who made as large a batch as possible with the small pot they borrowed. That was four great healing potions, and two small vials of what was leftover.

Meike cleaned their hands and took out the pamphlet from Joie. Some of these spells were far beyond their station as an apprentice mage, but it couldn't hurt to try.

The spell for communicating directly with animals highly appealed to them, for starters; it would be nice to pick Saffron's anxious brain, or have deep talks with Vivica. And parse Alek's babbling...

They were still poring over the spells when someone knocked at the door. "Letter for you," a gruff voice said.

"Coming!"

It was addressed to them in Moira's elegant handwriting.

You said you've got yourself a bear cub? Oh Meike...I don't fully approve, but what's done is done. At the very least, it'll make a grand companion when it's grown. Is

it a thornback bear, or one of the lesser varieties?
I've looked into those shrooms by the way, and they're
quite worthless. Absolute junk, I recommend tossing
or selling them, if you can find a good buyer.
Keep those stingers, though! The poison is quite vi-
able. I'd like to examine them personally, if you
don't mind...together?
And do let me know when you'll be back! Effie and
I miss you.

Meike shivered at the closing sentence. Effie, the demon goat, was certainly not a creature they wished to tango with. But they made sure to keep the stingers safe. A play date with Moira!

Hilarious enough, selling the potions was harder than getting rid of the junk—for a good price, that is. With it being a trading hub and all, there was no shortage of potion sellers, and they had far more prestige and wares than Meike had in one thumb.

Even so, they persevered, reluctantly agreeing to part with their stash for a paltry sum of two gold—and trading away the bulk of their mushroom bits. Meike told the man they were edible, and silently planned to make themself scarce before he got himself sick.

Overall, Meike made out with seventeen gold and forty-five silver coins. New armor and clothes would have to wait for now.

Meike lost that same five gold a half hour later, after spotting a cart of strange and exciting new herbs. They got enough to fill their satchel, as well as new recipes for some rather interesting potions.

"Shoot, I still need my spells..."

"Oi!" Further back in the crowd, they spotted Anniken's shock of white blonde hair. She was waving at them to come over, but ultimately forced her way through the crowd. "Got everything you need?"

"Um..." They patted the pamphlet in their bag. "I need to pick out spells, but I don't think I have enough for new armor. I think I went a little overboard, but I bought some new herbs to try out!"

"I told you, I know someone." She fingered their poncho. "But I can patch this up for you, maybe even stitch you some new gear. No point in you looking rough."

"But I won't be able to pay you!"

"Did I ask for money?"

"No, but—"

"Then don't worry about it." Anniken sniffed. "I'm allowed to take pride in my work. Would you like to grab a bite to eat? I can pay for your lunch."

Meike's stomach rumbled. They were holding out for dinner, but if she was offering... "Okay!"

Anniken took them to a quiet pub on the outskirts of Zachick and secured a private booth. The menu wasn't the greatest, but they had several vegetarian dishes for Meike.

They were happy to have a bowl of split pea soup and a tough hunk of bread. Anniken ordered a turkey leg and roasted potatoes.

"About these spells," she said, while Meike was gnawing at the bread. "You should opt for a good mix of supportive and offensive. Right now you have fireball and that magic light."

"I wanna learn all the elemental spells. Like ice!"

"Yes, yes, but what about this one?" She tapped the page. *Keen Edge*. Meike didn't need to read the description to know why Anniken would want it. "It's only fifty silver."

"I guess y'all do need buffs. I also like the binding spell." It said so on the page that a skilled mage could adapt the spell to suit their needs or aesthetics. Like a ring of thorns or chains around their target. "Ooh...or the Tempest Swarm!" Semi-sentient orbs of magic at their command? Yes, please!

"You sure about that? The binding spell is only one gold, but the Swarm is...five."

That left them with eleven gold...Meike groaned. "But I need spells!"

"You can take a fourth, but be wise about it."

"Then I'll take Hearing Aptitude." It wasn't offensive, flashy, or even cheap, but it had great potential.

Anniken shrugged. "It's your money," she said, but she looked pleased with herself.

With only nine gold left, Meike could only nod.

Meike doubled that nine gold into a respectable eighteen, only to lose most of it to tips and last minute purchases.

"It's been a pleasure doing business with you, Meike." Joie followed that up with a smile—all eyes—and bowed.

"Thanks," they said, lightly squeezing the wrapped book in their hands.

It was beautiful! The cover was an exquisite leather, the texture pleasing and soothing to the touch. Even better, every detail stood on its own; one could decipher the playful rabbits and foliage with the stroke of a finger.

"And here are those maps you requested."

Meike eagerly tucked the lot into their bag. The maps supposedly led to hidden quest areas. One simply couldn't stumble upon these; they needed to be directed.

They tipped Joie four gold coins for their hard work and craftsmanship, lowering their funds to eight. Six of those remaining coins went to Rickard.

"Oh, this is so cool!"

"Please, you're going to make me blush," he said, not exaggerating. "Would you like to give it a whirl?"

Meike tapped the tall, wooden staff against the ground, admiring the weight and feel. It looked not much different from what they expected of a normal staff, although if one looked closely, the wood steadily pulsed a dark blue. They felt it in their hands, even.

"I trust you," they said. That, and Meike didn't want to accidentally burn the whole market down. Anniken would never let them forget it.

"That's fine, but feel free to come to me, should you ever need adjustments. And for the final piece..."

Rickard performed a flourish of the hands, drawing pinkish swirls in the air. He curled both into fists and rested them, knuckles down, on the counter. "I took great care with these, as you'll be using them indefinitely."

Slowly, he revealed his hand—a series of magnificent wooden figures, carved into the likeness of the relevant animals: a bear, vines adorning its back, a wolf, and a little rabbit with floppy ears.

"Woah...." Meike gingerly picked up the mini Saffron and traced a finger down its spine. The wood was heavy in their palm, and cool to the touch, like stone. "This is really cool, Rickard."

"Please," he said, face redder than a strawberry. "I am an artist and take my requests quite seriously!"

"You did such a good job." The figurines came with their own pouch, built to withstand weather, moisture, and other incidents. "But how do I store my familiars in these?"

"With a summoning spell, of course!"

"Of course..." And they were currently too broke for that.

"What's so special about these maps? And how much did you spend on them?"

The others seemed intrigued, but Anniken was full of complaints.

"Two gold a piece, six for the lot."

"Six gold, for some ratty old maps?"

"They aren't ratty! Just well aged..." They assumed that was intentional, but it was hard to say.

"Oh, Meike..."

"You're just jealous you didn't find them first," Meike said, hands on their hips.

"That's not going to work on me."

Cass shooed Anniken aside and seized one of the maps. "These are pretty good, actually. Overpriced, but valuable."

"Overpriced..." But why would Joie overcharge? They seemed nice...

"Now, don't get down on yourself. You only overpaid for the..." She sighed. "Kobold mine. I know how to get there, but the other two are beyond me."

One was for an area that hosted crystal monsters, from deer to treants. The other was a canyon of slimes. Meike was less enthused about that one, but it was sure to have something of value.

"Let's do the mines," Pickles said. "Between me and Zel, we can clear the lot in under an hour. You and Cass can clean up."

"Now hold on, mutt. If we're doing this, it needs to be done right. Meike needs to upgrade their armor and train with their new staff, and...what else did you get?"

Meike held up the miniatures. "I need a summoning spell before I can use these."

"All the more reason to not charge in."

"I just need the money to buy a new spell. Unless you have a better idea."

Cass nodded, eyes closed. "Or I can just lend you the money. It's quicker."

"If you're sure..." And who knows how much *that* would cost?

"Relax, Meike. I trust that you'll pay it back later. I just don't want you running all over."

That solved one problem. "I want to swing by Laeford before we start questing."

"Take however long you need, but do be mindful of time constraints. You still need better gear."

"I want an auto-counter, too! I'm tired of being left out."

"But of course."

The price tag and ensuing debt dampened their spirits considerably, but.... Meike sighed and rubbed their temple. "I'll pay you back later."

Anniken shook her head. "Don't. Make me potions instead. Healing, poisons, anything that aids in solo combat."

"I can do that. I have some new recipes I want to try out."

"Is that why you're going back to Laeford? Everything you could want is right here."

"Zachick doesn't have a dedicated crafting space." Everyone came and went with the breeze. "And there's someone I want to see. Besides..."

There was more to Laeford than crafting stations, inns, and red bricked buildings.

"You don't need to explain it to me. Counters are hard to come across here, I'll admit."

"Are you coming along, too?"

"I'm considering it. There's more going on in the city, and we could always pick up some new quests."

"I'm down, but I'd like some non-combatant quests, too. Something relaxing, like foraging. I heard whispers of strange and unusual—well, to us—plants and fungi outside of the kingdom."

"Oh, I like the sound of that. It means new monsters, too."

Meike slowly blinked, like a cat. "Remember that we already have a new set of quests."

"Yeah, yeah. But Meike, do you realize how far those are?" She tapped an open map spread on their table. "I've checked, and only the mines are within Lexanard. And *that's* on the edge of the country."

They followed her finger. That was true...and neither of them had a map of the neighboring countries.

"Maybe it's good we stick around until I'm stronger."

"True. We'll want to retire the mule before we set out. It's only going to hold us back."

"But how will we transport our loot? Or rest during long travels?"

She couldn't expect everyone to travel on foot! It just wasn't sustainable.

"Which is why we'll get you a mount. Cass will figure something out, and we can get a saddlebag for Pickles. Or make him walk."

"A mount..." A horse like hers, or something unique to their interests?

"From Laeford. Let me worry about that." She rolled up the map and handed it back to Meike. "Focus on potion crafting. We're going to need a large batch, the biggest you can manage."

28

THE BINDING OF ALEK

SEASON 2 FINALE

"Why look who it is!" Moira didn't rush to embrace them, but she was smiling and her skin was radiant. That was as good a sign as any.

"Hey Moira! Look at what I've got." They held up a squirming Alek for her inspection. He was slowly outgrowing his harness and would need something bigger soon. "Aleksei, or Alek for short."

"Aw, he's simply precious." She waved and carefully extended a hand.

Alek pawed at the air, large clumsy movements. He uttered a soft grunt and wrapped his paw around her hand.

"Careful, Alek..."

"He's fine. They can't do much damage at this age." She giggled when he nibbled on her finger. "See? He's just curious."

"Actually, I had a question about that."

"About bears?" She carefully extracted her hand. "I'm not an expert, but I'll do what I can. You may have better luck at the library."

"I still need a library card…" Meike never had time to do so before, and definitely not now. "I wanted to ask someone I trust." They glanced away. "I need help with my summoning spell."

Moira's eyes lit up. "A summoning spell, you say?"

"Yeah! I even got some of those fancy figures. I have three, carved from a magical wood."

"Oh! Like Effie?"

Grinning, Meike fished out the intricately carved figures. "I named the wolf Vivica, she's my heavy hitter."

"Vivica…" Moira took the figures one by one, admiring each individual marking. "These are impressive. Did you commission these from Rickard of Zachick?"

"How did you know?"

"Not too many people in Lexanard can make such a catalyst. Which is a shame, as it's in such high demand. I keep asking him to move his shop to Laeford, where he'll be better protected and garner higher profits, but he turns me down every time."

"Is that where you got Effie's?"

"No, Madame Claudette referred me to a local. Rickard has the better rates, but he's too far to justify the travel."

"You could send someone for you."

"I'd rather go myself or not at all. But this isn't about me. Come, let's go to my place."

"There is something else I wanted to ask," Meike said, as they climbed the short flight of stairs to her apartment. "It's about—do you know what an auto-counter is?"

"Of course! I think I still have mine, actually. I call it a PDA though. Auto-counter is too clunky."

"It lets you know what it is. It's convenient."

"Yes, well…if you want it, you can have it."

"Really? You're just going to give it to me?" What's the catch?

"Why not? I don't have a need for one, and they're awfully expensive these days."

Their own auto-counter! The version Moira offered was an older model, the design reminiscent of those pocket devices with virtual pets, but it worked.

"How does this..."

"You can play with it later." Moira waved them into the kitchenette, the table lined with a series of beakers, tubes, and all matters of scientific equipment. "Sorry, I wasn't expecting company."

"It's alright, I surprised you."

"No worries. Get settled while I clear this off."

Meike sank onto the couch, expecting to wait a good ten to fifteen minutes, but Moira waved a hand and the items whizzed through the air and into their respective cabinets. Everything sorted itself with gentle, rhythmic clacks that Meike found oddly soothing.

"How'd you do that?" And how could they emulate it?

"Magic," she said, with a little flip of her hair. "Now, come here and set little Alek down, next to his token."

Token. An interesting choice of words, but Meike rolled with it.

"It's alright, boy. We're just going to put you in a playpen." They gave him one last hug and placed him on the center of the table.

Moira took his token and scratched it against the table, as if lighting a match. But rather than flame, the wood pulsed with strange markings—a circle and a rough star drawn in the middle.

"I'll do this just once, and then you're on your own. We'll start with a binding spell."

A binding spell...they kissed him on the head and set him down. "It'll be alright, Alek."

The cub issued a series of whimpers, but otherwise remained seated on the pentagon.

"He's going to cry," Moira said. "Don't be alarmed, and don't lose focus."

"It's not going to hurt him, is it?"

Moira sighed and bowed her head. "It may sting a little, but binding is generally...unpleasant for the receiver."

Other than Nancy from The Craft, Meike couldn't envision what else that may look like. And in that case, the character was very resistant to the act, and responded with aggression before eventually being subdued. Alek was calm, if a little shaken.

"What's the chant?"

She took Meike's hands and held them tight. "I bind you, Alek."

"I bind you, Alek."

He jolted upright with a borderline human sob, the pentagon glowing and flickering in the dim light. Meike asked about candles, but Moira dismissed it as meaningless theatrics.

"I bind you to the token."

Meike repeated the words. The bear figurine lightly rattled against the tabletop.

"Under my service, forever, till we part."

"Till we part," Meike said, as Alek lurched forward. He bounced back when he reached the edge of the circle.

"I bind you, to call upon as I see fit."

Alek ran into the edge once more, and again went sprawling into the middle, where he groaned and clawed at the wood. The pentagon shone brightly beneath him, flickering like a flame and gravitating to his fur, where it latched and held him in place.

"Moira—"

She hissed. "Don't break the circle! I bind you, Alek! Say it!"

"I bind you, Alek!"

Completely consumed by the symbol, Alek was twisted and warped into a spectral clone, dragged towards the hovering token. He uttered one last squeal and was sucked into the mouth of the tiny token.

Meike shivered as token's eyes briefly lit a vivid cerulean. "Is it done?"

But Moira held tight to their hand. "Don't, the ritual isn't finished!"

The token's eyes turned crimson, and the figure itself began to shiver and shake.

"Alek!"

"He's fine. This is a test to see if the spell took."

The token rolled back and forth, occasionally righting itself, only to fall over and spin in tight circles. Meike could do nothing but stand by and watch in silence until the token came to a stop for a solid two minutes.

The eyes glowed a dull purple, and with a soft pop, emitted a thin stream of blueish smoke.

"Now you may," Moira said.

Meike carefully picked up the token by the sides, and winced from the searing hot heat. But they held tight long enough to drop it into the palm of their hand. The token steadily throbbed, like a miniature heart.

"How do I get him out again?"

"You don't," she said. "At least not for the next few days."

"Days? Won't he get sad?" Poor Alek, locked away for hours at a time...

"No. When they're put away like that, the mind shuts down to protect their mental state. It's a form of hibernation."

"Hibernation..." Meike flexed their hand around the token and set it down. It left a rough burn mark in their palm, and stung, but if Alek could bear it, so could they. "I have two other familiars to bind." They weren't fond of the term, but hated the idea of calling it mere storage.

"You can do the rabbit on your own, but I'll help you subdue Vivica. It's been a while since I've handled larger creatures, but between the two of us, anything is possible."

"I really appreciate it, Moira. I couldn't have done it without you."

"Oh hush," she said. "And let me see to your wound."

They protested at first, but quickly acquiesced to Moira's firm nature and gentle hands.

"What are you..."

"Aloe vera," she said. A simple gelatinous cream, light green and slimy. The texture was horrible, but the combination of her careful caresses and the naturally cool cream worked to placate them. The pain rapidly diminished, leaving only her touch and the refreshing scent and tingle of mint.

"Better?"

"Yeah," they murmured. "I think I'd like to learn that recipe for myself and my adventuring group."

"One thing at a time, Meike!" She smiled, eyes down turned as she held their hand. "I would be willing to help you in other ways."

"With potions?"

"That too."

Meike gently pried their hand free; it was more human contact than they usually tolerated, even if she was one of the nicer ones.

"Right, the auto counter!"

"Ha, that old thing." She chuckled, brushing hair from her face. "It's all yours."

They could've hugged her, right then and there, but remained firmly rooted in their seat. "Thanks again, Moira. I'll take good care of it!"

"Don't thank me yet," she said. "I'll help you program it later, but for now." She leaned back in her seat with a sigh. "Let's take care of that wolf of yours."

Saffron went with little complaint, accepting his fate like a man lined up at the guillotine. But Vivica...

"Okay, this isn't going to be easy," Moira said, on the other side of the circle. She'd drawn a large one on the roof of her apartment, and summoned Effie to cover another gap, leaving Meike to manage their own corner.

They really would've liked to have two additional spellcasters instead of the goat, but it couldn't be helped right now.

Vivica paced the confines of the pentagram, sniffing the edge of the chalk marks. She raised her head and neatly pulled her lips from her teeth, exposing a nasty set of fangs. To say she was displeased put it mildly.

"We're going to do what we did before, but I trust you to do this alone."

"Alone? Moira, I can't!"

"You can and you will," she snapped. "You performed just fine with Saffron."

"Yeah, but he's a bunny! Vivica..."

At the sound of her name, Vivica turned and fixed those cold gray eyes on Meike. They gulped.

"She's in the circle," Moira said. "She's *contained*. And once you begin the chant, she can't get out. Now, stop complaining and get into position."

Meike groaned, but did as instructed. "I'm sorry, girl," they said, and launched into the incantation. They'd recited it so many times while prepping that it came to them naturally.

"I bind you, Vivica. I bind you to the token. Under my service, forever, until we part."

Her lip curled, but Vivica didn't pounce or move an inch from her current position. And somehow, that bitter resignation stung more than anything.

"I bind you!"

29

SOMETHING TO CRY ABOUT

"**M**eike!"

"Oh, darn it," they said in horror.

Vivica's eyes narrowed as a fresh growl rumbled in her throat.

"Easy, girl. Easy…"

"Meike, complete the binding, quick!"

"I bind—"

But the light of the pentagon dimmed, the markings suddenly faded and graying at the edges.

"Shit shit shit, Effie!"

Meike dove out of the way, hands cupped protectively over their head. A heavy paw struck them on the back, and a set of jaws wrapped around their arm. They didn't register the pain at first, or even their own shrieks, only the frenzied growling in their ear.

"Effie! Effie, make her stop!"

The pressure on their body eased, evoking a cry from Meike. They clasped a hand over the searing pain in their arm, eyes screwed shut to avoid seeing whatever damage their familiar caused.

"Meike…" Soft arms tentatively rested on their sides. "You're going to be okay. Let's get you inside, alright?"

They shook their head.

"Meike, honey, please. You're hurt…"

"You said it would be fine," they mumbled.

"It was a mistake. You almost had it."

"Where is she?"

Moira squeezed their shoulders. "Effie has her. Please, let's go inside. We can try again later."

"I'm sorry," they said, blinking back stinging tears. Why did they mess everything up?

"Shh, I've got you."

Meike tried not to cry as Moira ferried them downstairs, but the tears flowed regardless, bitter and heavy and full of salt.

"Where is she," they said, as Moira helped them out of their poncho. The fabric was ruined in the back and side. Nothing Anniken couldn't patch up, but it was a shame. She'd worked so hard on it, too!

"Vivica is safe, don't worry."

"I need to know now!" Meike sucked in a low breath as Moira peeled back their sleeve. "I know she's upset—she must feel so betrayed right now—I'd at least like to apologize."

"For what," she snapped. "Meike, she could've killed you. If I wasn't there, she would have."

"No, she wouldn't do that! We're friends."

"Friends…do you want to take this off, or should I cut it off you?"

"Cut? No, I'll…" They raised their arms and froze in place, pain radiating from their injuries. "Ah, it hurts…"

"Here, allow me..." Moira carefully sheared off the sleeve with a pair of scissors, and pressed it against the nasty marks on their arm. One glance was enough for Meike, who didn't recognize the inflamed skin. "Hold this. I need to get some fresh water and prepare a poultice."

"Can't I just have a potion?"

"No, Meike...not everything warrants a quick fix."

"But—" Why not, when potions were so easily accessible? They carried potions at all times for injuries such as this. It was necessary on the field and just as much in everyday life.

Moira returned with a shallow bowl of water and two rags. She dipped one rag into the water, holding it there for a few seconds, and then wrung it out. "Are you so reliant on magic that you can't appreciate gentler remedies? Where are you off in a hurry to?" She pressed the rag—pleasantly warm and damp—against Meike's flesh.

They caught themself sighing in relief and even dared a peek at their arm. It was still bad, the brown skin a dull red in places, but it was cleaner now. "What's wrong with instant healing? Why draw out the pain?"

"It's not about drawing it out. You want the body to heal naturally, to remind you of your humanity." She dipped the rag again, and tended to the more stubborn gashes, drawing out sluggish tendrils of blood. Meike winced and looked away. "I've seen it happen, time and time again. Adventurers develop a complex that leaves them to believe they're invincible—as long as they have a steady supply of potions."

"Is that really such a bad thing," they said, accepting the dry rag. "It's a good business model for us too, remember?"

"Oh, I'm not arguing that we shouldn't support our clients. It's over-reliance that has me concerned. Especially simple matters like these. You wouldn't use a potion to heal a hanged nail or stubbed toe, would you?"

"No, but those are small wounds."

"So is this bite," she said, and opened a packet of herbs. The earthy aroma filled Meike's nostrils and instilled them with a sense of ease. "If it was nastier, I'd consider it, but it doesn't look that bad. These will heal on their own."

"That's good! I knew she wouldn't kill me. She was just scared..."

"Shh..." She applied the poultice, a greenish mix that looked funny on Meike's skin. "We'll clean this off in thirty minutes, after it hardens. I don't think you'll need stitches, but I'd like to wrap the wound before I send you home."

"Thanks, doctor Moira." They flashed her a cheery smile.

"Don't thank me yet," she said, tugging on the back of their tunic. "I have to make sure she didn't get you here."

Thankfully, any wounds Meike had on their back were superficial. Moira treated those with a simple wipe down and applied stinging witch hazel.

"And Vivica?"

"She's been contained," Moira said, wrapping a bandage up the length of Meike's arm. "You need to give her space right now, and I definitely wouldn't recommend binding her. Not when she's in a volatile state."

"I get that, but I still want to see her."

Moira sighed and leaned her head back. "Effie!"

The goat-like familiar appeared seconds later, causing Meike to jolt upright. "Yes, mistress?"

"Where's the wolf?"

"I placed her in a crate, as instructed."

"See? Contained."

They glared at Effie. "How big is the crate?"

"Adequately sized, for a wolf of her build. She's quite unhappy with the arrangement, but she's since calmed down. She was napping, last I checked."

"And where is this crate?"

"In a safe place, worry not."

"Moira..."

"Meike, relax. Effie won't allow harm to befall your pet. We just think it's wise to separate you two for the moment."

"Fine," they said, and started to rub their arm, before remembering the bandage. "How long do I have to wear these?"

"I'd personally leave them on overnight, but you can remove them after a few hours. The wounds should be sealed by then."

They tentatively patted their arm and winced. No, not quite ready yet. "Thanks again, Moira! I'll come back for Vivica later, I guess."

"Yes, get some rest. We can try again in a few days."

"I need to do it before I leave...but I need potions first. Lots and lots of potions!"

"And I'll help you, but please, rest first."

That was easy for her to say; Meike couldn't imagine cozying up now, or even sleeping. But they were tired and ashamed, and in no position to argue.

Tomorrow was another day, after all.

"Thanks again, Moira."

"'Scuse me, ma'am!"

Anniken peered at the dirty street urchin with disdain. He wore a mud streaked tunic and leggings with artful tears. Interesting combination, that. Her eyes lingered on the rolls of parchment in his satchel. "What do you want, kid?"

"Only your time and consideration." He flashed her a rather charming smile, teeth almost perfect but for the large two front teeth. If he cleaned up and did something with his windswept hair, he could be the perfect model.

She tentatively accepted the proffered flyer. "What exactly are you pushing?"

He cleared his throat and clasped his hands together. "For the better treatment of our beloved canine friends. There's an abandoned district where wild dogs roam free, and there's been talk of tearing it down altogether, but we believe it would be more beneficial to convert this area into a dog sanctuary—"

"I'll sign your damn petition. Do you have a pen?"

The lad's eyes sparkled. "Yes, ma'am! Thank you kindly, ma'am!"

Anniken scribbled a hasty signature and passed the form back. She had a soft spot for dogs, even dirty old mutts like Pickles. And if it would keep strays off the streets...

"Good luck, kid."

The boy scrambled off, a wide smile on his face, while Anniken settled for something far more grim.

She had a lot on her mind as of late, most of which involved Laken, her beloved and untamed Knight. And then there was that favor she owed Meike...

Kind, good natured Meike, who lagged behind in major milestones and overall maturity. They had the potential to be someone of great importance, but fell into the trap of creature comforts and odd obsessions. First fungi, and now bear cubs...where did it end?

Her mind shifted back to Laken, as it was wont to do as of late. And where had she gone wrong there?

Anniken clenched her fist around the hilt of her sword. No. Laken alone was to blame. Anniken's crime was allowing them in. That made being the first one to reach out sharper than the cold steel at her hip.

In the confines of her rented room, Anniken reminded herself that this was strictly business and nothing more. Direct contact was the fastest option, but she saw or heard Laken's responses, her resolve would falter. No, written correspondence was the only way to shield herself.

> *Laken,*
>
> *I have a request for you, if you're willing to entertain it. It concerns a quest I and others are on. Meike, my mage friend, is among our number. I'm sure you remember them. We'll be swinging by the capital and can talk more then.*
>
> *- Zelamir*

Brief and to the point.

Anniken sealed the letter with her customary signature, a stylized Z for Zelamir. It meant nothing to the masses, but Laken would understand. Especially when she received it via Priority Pigeon.

Afterword

Thanks for reading! Last Train Home is an ongoing web serial. You can find some fun tidbits on my site: siennaeggler.com/last-train-home

The current story is up to season four, and the second book will be released upon its completion. So if you absolutely cannot wait for the second book, I strongly recommend following along online. And for those interested in seeing more POVs from Anniken, seasons three and four properly introduce Anniken as the secondary MC I always intended her to be. I may or may not do some for the side characters, or save them for special "between seasons" bits, such as the Harvest Side Stories.

I've teased a bit of romance between several characters, mainly Anniken and Laken at the moment, who have an "on and off again" thing going on. However, I have a very slow burn romance planned for Meike and Moira. Meike is currently too focused on their studies and questing to even consider the notion of romance (they're AroAce), so don't expect fireworks on their end. Moira is more of a romantic, which will be a fun realization for Meike.

Anyway, Long Train Home is a story I've been dabbling with over the years, originally inspired by the Log Horizon series. I'm excited to share it with y'all, as I have a lot planned for this series! Much of that involves alchemy, magic, and yes, magitech! This is a passion project of mine that's designed to be a mix of slice of life, crafting and gathering, and questing. This is the only long series I can really see myself doing, as it has countless potential and is suitable for a broad audience.

I'd love to design my own site for it at some point, but that will have to come later. Just getting the story out into the world is my main priority, along with book covers and some official character art.

Til next time!

About the Author

Sienna Eggler is a queer and autistic author with a love for campy body horror, black comedy, and supernatural creatures such as shifters and vampires. Ey primarily write fantasy and science fiction, with bits of horror sprinkled throughout.

When not writing, ey like to play indie adventure games, visual novels, and pine over sapphic vampires. Ey live with eir partner and three cats.

You can learn more about em on eir blog at www.siennaegg ler.com/, where you can subscribe to eir newsletter for updates and news about future books.